总 顾 问　李赋宁　胡壮麟
总 主 编　黄必康
网络版主编　李建华

根据教育部最新颁布《大学英语课程教学要求》编写

Student's Book

COLLEGE
BASIC ENGLISH

学生用书

大学英语基础教程 3

主编　曹杰旺

副主编　梁亚平　高玉兰　郑晓行
编　者　方秀才　张　琦　姜艳艳

北京大学出版社
PEKING UNIVERSITY PRESS

图书在版编目(CIP)数据

大学英语基础教程(3)学生用书 / 曹杰旺主编. —北京：北京大学出版社，2009.8
(大学英语立体化网络化系列教材)
ISBN 978-7-301-15478-6

Ⅰ.大… Ⅱ.曹… Ⅲ.英语–高等学校–教材 Ⅳ.H31

中国版本图书馆 CIP 数据核字(2009)第 116548 号

书　　　名：大学英语基础教程(3)学生·用书
著作责任者：曹杰旺　主编
策　　　划：张　冰
责 任 编 辑：黄瑞明
标 准 书 号：ISBN 978-7-301-15478-6/H·2287
出 版 发 行：北京大学出版社
地　　　址：北京市海淀区成府路 205 号　　100871
网　　　址：http://www.pup.cn
电　　　话：邮购部 62752015　发行部 62750672　编辑部 62767315　出版部 62754962
电 子 邮 箱：zbing@pup.pku.edu.cn
印 刷 者：北京大学印刷厂
经 销 者：新华书店
　　　　　　787毫米×1092毫米　16 开本　11.75 印张　270 千字
　　　　　　2009 年 8 月第 1 版　2009 年 8 月第 1 次印刷
定　　　价：25.00 元 (配有光盘)

总　序

　　新世纪之初,我国的大学英语教学正面临着一个新的起点:提升英语听说能力,走向英语实际运用。这是一个立足于社会现实,尊重语言社会功能的学习视界。知识经济的到来,信息社会的产生,全球化的趋势,多元文化的共存,这些人类现象共同构筑了我们今天的社会现实,而英语作为国际通用语言,正是一个国家或个人有效地参与国际竞争和文化交往的重要工具。而最能表现语言的工具性质的,莫过于在语言的实际运用过程中了。

　　英语教材的不断更新和建设历来都是促进大学英语教学改革,提高教学质量的先行任务。目前,国家教育部和全国高校外语教学指导委员会坚定推行大学英语教学改革,制定颁布了新时期的《大学英语课程教学要求》,为新的大学英语教材的编写提供了指导依据,同时也显示了编写新的大学英语教材的必要性和紧迫性。正是在此情势下,北京大学教材建设委员会重点立项"大学英语"教材建设,北京大学出版社具体组织、策划了本套"大学英语立体化网络化系列教材"的编写和出版工作。

　　本套教材被评为普通高等教育"十一五"国家级规划教材,根据《大学英语课程教学要求》,我们又在原书基础上进行了修订。

　　北京大学教材建设委员会将本套教材列为重点教材建设项目,重点支持。我国英语教学研究权威李赋宁教授、胡壮麟教授担任本套教材总顾问,北京大学英语系黄必康教授任总主编,中国农业大学外语系李建华教授任网络版主编。

　　编写过程中我们也得到了各主编所在院校的大力支持和配合,得到了北京大学、北京师范大学、北京航空航天大学、中国农业大学、复旦大学、南京大学、北京交通大学、中山大学、吉林大学、东南大学、大连理工大学、华南理工大学、东北大学、四川大学、重庆大学、云南大学、河北师范大学、西安电子科技大学、山东农业大学、西北师范大学、长春师范学院、山东青年管理干部学院、淮南师范学院、江西财经大学、西北大学、福州大学等院校数十位专家教授的关注和支持,对此我们深表谢忱。我们也特别感谢本系列教材几十位中外英语教学专家在编写过程中认真细致,富有成效的工作!

　　中国大学英语改革任重道远,大学英语教材建设未有止境。本套大学英语系列教材既循改革步伐,探索教学新路,缺点与不足乃至谬误之处在所难免。衷心希望得到专家学者的批评指正,听到广大师生的改进意见。

大学英语立体化网络化系列教材

Acknowledgements

We are indebted, mainly for the reading selections, to many sources. We have put forth the fullest effort to trace each and every source, and their origins and our acknowledgements are indicated within the book. However, a small number of copyright materials remain uncredited because the original copyright holders could not be located, or we were unable to establish communication with them. It may be the case that some unintentional omissions have occurred in the employment of some copyright materials. We are grateful to these authors and sources, and we apologize for not being able to extend our acknowledgements in detail. For any questions concerning copyrights and permissions, please contact

Copyrights Department
Peking University Press
Beijing, 100871
P. R. China
Telephone: +86 10 62752036
Fax: +86 10 62556201
Email: xiena@pup.pku.edu.cn

We are much obliged for any information concerned and will make necessary arrangements for the appropriate settlement of any possible copyright issue.

Contents

Unit 1

PART I PREPARATORY

WORDS IN CONTEXT

Read aloud the following sentences, paying attention to the meaning of the words in italics.

1. Mike *insisted* that he was right.

2. It's a question of *disciplining* yourself to write everyday.

3. The rent was much more than we had *expected* to pay.

4. You *startled* me! I didn't hear you come in.

5. Fletcher's fitness and *superior* technique brought him victory.

6. With one or two *exceptions*, there are few women teachers here.

7. Fluency in three languages *qualifies* her for work in the big company.

8. First impressions really *count*.

9. *Despite* all our efforts to save the school, the County decided to close it.

10. Good food and plenty of exercise are *essential* for a healthy life.

Write the meaning of each of the following words in the corresponding blank. You can write either in English or in Chinese.

insist _____

discipline _____

expect _____

startle _____

superior _____

exception _____

qualify _____

count _____

despite _____

essential _____

EXPRESSIONS IN CONTEXT

Study the following expressions and see how they are used in sentences.

turn out to be 原来是，结果

◇ What we teach our children is what they turn out to be.

seem to 似乎

◇ Well, they seem to make a good couple.

take pains 尽心竭力做某事；小心谨慎做某事

◇ He took pains to present a smart, efficient appearance.

calm down (使)安静下来

◇ It was difficult to calm down the football fans.

break the record 破纪录

◇ She outdid herself to break the record she had set.

at the moment 此刻,目前

◇ He was the only person awake at the moment.

be startled to 吃惊

◇ My mother was startled to know the news.

add ... to... 增加,增添

◇ Your coming added much fun to the party.

EXPRESSIONS LEARNED IN DISPLAY

Complete each of the following sentences with the expressions you have just learned.

1. We _____ have wandered from the path.

2. Your words _____ some evidence _____ the case.

3. You should _____ more _____ with your work.

4. She is terribly excited. We must try to _____ her _____ .

5. Our chief concern _____ is the weather.

6. Keep your finger crossed that I'll _____ .

7. The teacher _____ see his performance.

8. That guy we met _____ Maria's cousin.

PART II LANGUAGE IN CONTEXT

GET YOURSELF INTERESTED

Read the following summary in Chinese and think what you are going to read in this text.

> 奥林匹克运动会是人类伟大的运动盛事，在奥运会上赢得金牌也成为了运动员们最想实现的梦想。然而在 1936 年柏林举办的奥运会上，两个陌生人之间的友情却战胜了获取金牌的渴望。本文讲述了竞争、胜利和友情的感人故事。

PREVIEW QUESTIONS

Work in pairs or groups and discuss the following questions.

1. Do you love sports? What sports activities do you often take part in?

2. What do you know about Olympic Games?

3. Which athlete do you like most?

4. Do you agree with the famous saying "a great man cannot brook a rival"? Why?

READING SELECTION

Text A

My Greatest Olympic Prize

It was the summer of 1936. The Olympic Games were being held in Berlin. Because Adolf

Hitler childishly insisted that his performers were members of a "master race," nationalistic feelings were at an all-time high.

I wasn't too worried about all this. I'd trained, sweated and disciplined myself for six years, 5 with the Games in mind. While I was going over on the boat, all I could think about was taking home one or two of those gold medals. I had my eyes especially on the running broad jump. A year before, as a sophomore at the Ohio State, I'd set the world's record of 26 feet 8 1/4 inches. Nearly everyone expected me to win this event.

When the time came for the broad-jump trials, I was startled to see a tall boy hitting the pit 10 at almost 26 feet on his practice leaps! He turned out to be a German named Luz Long. I was told that Hitler hoped to win the jump with him.

I guessed that if Long won, it would add some new support to the Nazis' "master race" theory. After all, I am a Negro. Angry about Hitler's ways, I determined to go out there and really show Dear Fuhrer and his master race who was superior and who wasn't.

15 An angry athlete is an athlete who will make mistakes, as any coach will tell you. I was no exception. On the first of my three qualifying jumps, I leaped from several inches beyond the take-off board for a foul. On the second jump, I fouled even worse.

Walking a few yards from the pit, I 20 kicked disgustedly at the dirt. Suddenly I felt a hand on my shoulder. I turned to look into the friendly blue eyes of the tall German broad jumper. He had easily qualified for the finals on his first attempt. He offered me a firm 25 handshake.

"Jesse Owens, I'm Luz Long. I don't think we've met." He spoke English well, though with a German twist to it.

"Glad to meet you," I said. Then, trying

childishly /'tʃaɪldɪʃli/ *adv.* 天真地;幼稚地
insist /ɪn'sɪst/ *v.* 坚持,坚持认为
nationalistic /ˌnæʃənə'lɪstɪk/ *adj.* 民族(国家主义的)
discipline /'dɪsɪplɪn/ *v.* 严格要求自己;约束自己
broad jump 跳远
sophomore /'sɒfəmɔː/ *n.* (中等、专科学校或大学的)二年级学生
expect /ɪk'spekt/ *v.* 预料,希望
trial /'traɪəl/ *n.* 测试,试验
startle /'stɑːtl/ *v.* 使大吃一惊
pit /pɪt/ *n.* 深坑
turn out to be 结果是,原来是
exception /ɪk'sepʃən/ *n.* 例外
qualify /'kwɒlɪfaɪ/ *v.* (使)具有资格,(使)合格
take-off 起跳
board /bɔːd/ *n.* 板,牌子
foul /faʊl/ *v.* 〈体〉(对……)犯规;*n.* 犯规
kick /kɪk/ *v.* 踢
disgustedly /dɪs'gʌstɪdli/ *adv.* 厌恶地
dirt /dɜːt/ *n.* 泥土;污垢
twist /twɪst/ *n.* 弯曲;扭歪

to hide my nervousness, I added, "How are you?"

"I'm fine. The question is: How are you?"

"What do you mean?" I asked.

"Something must be eating you," he said—proud the way foreigners are when they've mastered a bit of American slang. "You should be able to qualify with your eyes closed."

"Believe me, I know it," I told him—and it felt good to say that to someone.

For the next few minutes we talked together. I didn't tell Long what was "eating" me, but he seemed to understand my anger, and he took pains to reassure me. Finally, seeing that I had calmed down somewhat, he pointed to the take-off board.

"Look," he said. "Why don't you draw a line a few inches behind the board and aim at
making your take-off from there? You'll be sure not to foul, and you certainly ought to jump far enough to qualify. What does it matter if you're not first in the trials? Tomorrow is what counts."

Suddenly all the tension seemed to leave my body as the truth of what he said hit me. Confidently, I drew a line a full foot behind the hoard and proceeded to jump from there. I qualified with almost a foot to spare.

That night I walked over to Luz Long's room in the Olympic village to thank him. We sat and talked for two hours—about track and field, ourselves, the world situation, a dozen other things. When I finally got up to leave, we both knew that a real friendship had been formed. Luz would go out to the field the next day trying to beat me if he could. But I knew that he wanted me to do my best—even if that meant my winning.

As it turned out, Luz broke his own past record. In doing so, he pushed me on to a peak performance. I remember that at the instant I landed from my final jump—the one which set the Olympic record of 26 feet 5 1/16 inches—he was at
my side, congratulating me. Despite the fact that Hitler glared at us from the stands not a hundred

slang /slæŋ/ **n.** 俚语

take pains 尽心竭力做某事;小心谨慎做某事

reassure /ˌriːəˈʃʊə/ **v.** (使)消除恐惧或疑虑;恢复信心

proceed to **v.** 接着做某事

peak /piːk/ **adj.** 最高点的,最高水平的

at the instant 一……就……

glare at 用(愤怒的)目光注视

stand /stænd/ **n.** 看台,观众席

yards away, Luz shook my hand—and it wasn't a fake "smile with a broken heart" sort of grip, either.

60 All the gold medals and cups I have wouldn't make a plating on the 24-carat friendship I felt for Luz Long at the moment. I realized then that Luz was just what Pierre de Coubertin, founder of the modern Games, must have had in his mind when he said, "The important thing in the Olympic Games is not winning but taking part. The essential thing in life is not conquering but fighting well."

> fake /feɪk/ *adj.* 假的，冒充的
> grip /ɡrɪp/ *n.* 紧握；紧咬；阵痛
> plating /'pleɪtɪŋ/ *n.* 电镀；被覆金属
> carat /'kærət/ *n.* 开(黄金纯度单位)
> at the moment 此刻，目前
> have sth/sb in mind 心中考虑到某物／某人
> essential /ɪ'senʃəl/ *adj.* 必不可少的；非常重要的

COMPREHENSION CHECK

Understanding the General Ideas

Discuss the following questions in pairs or groups. The key words given in the brackets may help you in your discussion.

1. When and where did the story take place?

   (summer, 1936, Berlin, Olympic Games)

2. What happened on the author's qualifying jumps?

   (first, leap, foul, beyond take-off board, second, worse)

3. How did Luz Long help the author?

   (understand, take pains, reassure)

4. Who set the Olympic record and won the gold medal?

   (Jesse Owens, set the Olympic record of 26 feet 5 1/16 inches)

5. Why dose the author think of the Olympic prize he won in Berlin as the greatest one?

   (important thing, winning, taking part)

7

Understanding the Specifics

Read the following sentences and tell if they are true or false according to the text. In the brackets leading each statement, put "T" for true or "F" for false.

1. (　　) Jesse Owens was very worried because of Adolph Hitler.

2. (　　) Jesse Owens had set the world's record as a sophomore.

3. (　　) Jesse Owens fouled on his three qualifying jumps.

4. (　　) Jesse Owens fouled because of nervousness.

5. (　　) With the help of Luz Long, Jesse Owens qualified for the finals.

6. (　　) Luz set the Olympic record of 26 feet 5 1/16 inches.

7. (　　) Luz congratulated Jesse sincerely though Hitler was very angry.

8. (　　) A real friendship was formed between Jesse Owens and Luz Long even though they were rivals.

STUDY AND PRACTICE

Vocabulary

Fill in the blanks with the words below. Change the form where necessary.

insist	discipline	expect	startle	superior
exception	qualify	count	despite	essential

1. Food is _____ for life.

2. The test showed he was the _____ player.

3. Let's _____ the people who are present.

4. I will have another glass if you _____.

5. At least I'm not afraid of _____ my kids.

6. I yelled in my dream, which _____ my roommate out of his sleep.

7. Our four-week course will _____ you to teach English overseas.

8. This is considered an _____ to the rule.

9. The ascent of the mountain is proceeding as _____.

10. _____ the fact that she is short, she is an excellent basketball player.

Expressions

Rewrite the following sentences with help of the phrases and expressions provided. The italicized part in each sentence may serve as the hint for your task. The first sentence is done for you.

turn out to be	seem to	take pains	calm down
have sth in mind	at the moment	proceed to	glare at

1. We are short of water and food *now*.

   We are short of water and food at the moment.

2. The cowboy finally manages *to make* their cattle *stay quiet*.

   _____

3. I hope everything will *become* all right *at last*.

   _____

4. Your lips *are likely to* become blue with cold.

   _____

9

5. We must *try our best* to ensure the safty of the people.

_____

6. Patrick said he liked my work, and then *continued to* tell me everything was

wrong with it.

_____

7. Don't *look at* your teacher *angrily*. You deserved the scolding.

_____

8. It's a nice house, but it wasn't quite what we *had been thinking of*.

_____

Translation

A From Chinese to English

1. 她坚持认为自己是无罪的。

2. 他说的那番话后来证明是一派胡言。

3. 这项法律适用于所有欧洲国家,英国也不例外。

4. 警察就在爆炸的那个时刻赶到了。

5. 他的承诺并无多大价值。

6. 你似乎对广州颇为熟悉。

7. 中国运动员在跨栏比赛中创造了一项新的世界纪录。

8. 我们队有参加第二轮比赛的资格吗?

B From English to Chinese

1. An angry athlete is an athlete who will make mistakes, as any coach will tell you.

2. On the first of my three qualifying jumps, I leaped from several inches beyond the take-off board for a foul.

3. I didn't tell Long what was "eating" me, but he seemed to understand my anger, and he took pains to reassure me.

4. As it turned out, Luz broke his own past record.

5. I remember that at the instant I landed from my final jump—the one which set the Olympic record of 26 feet 5 1/16 inches—he was at my side, congratulating me.

GRAMMAR

Commparative Degrees of Adjectives and Adverbs (形容词和副词的比较级)(I)

1. 基本概念

当形容词、副词出现在句中时,它们有三种语法形式:原来形式称为原级(Positive Degree),表示一个事物或人比另一事物或人"更……"的形容词或副词称为比较级(Comparative Degree),表示在 3 个或更多事物或人中"最……"的形容词或副词称为最高级(Superlative Degree)。

2. 比较级和最高级的构成法

1) 形容词

(1) 单音节形容词

单音节形容词通常都以加 -er 和 -est 的方式构成其比较级和最高级;以 -e 结尾

的词,只加 -r 和 -st;一般说来,以一个的辅音字母结尾的单音节词,末尾字母要双写,再加 -er 和 -est;以"辅音+y"结尾的词,变 y 为 i 再加 -er 和 -est:

tall	taller	tallest
large	larger	largest
hot	hotter	hottest
busy	busier	busiest

（2）多音节形容词

多音节形容词通常加 more 和 most；但双音节形容词有时也以加词尾方式构成比较级和最高级：

more beautiful	most beautiful
more lucky	most lucky
happier	happiest

（3）不规则变化

原级	比较级	最高级
good(well)	better	best
bad(ill,evil)	worse	worst
many(much)	more	most
little	less(lesser)	least
old	older(elder)	oldest(eldest)
late	later(latter)	latest(last)
far	farther(further)	farthest(furthest)
near	nearer	nearest(next)

2）副词

（1）单音节副词和单音节形容词一样,都以加 -er,-est 的方式构成比较级和最高级。

（2）双音节副词,特别是以 -ly 结尾的,大多加 more 和 most:wisely, more wisely, most wisely

（3）不规则变化

原级	比较级	最高级
well	better	best
badly(ill)	worse	worst
much	more	most
little	less	least
late	later(latterly)	latest(last)
far	farther(further)	farthest(furthest)
near	nearer	nearest(next)

（4）less (least)+形容词(或副词)

less 和 least 可加在各类音节的词前表示"较不……"或"最不……"：

small   less small   least small

beautiful   less beautiful   least beautiful

This house is less beautiful(不如……美) than yours.

This house is the least beautiful(最不美) of all.

IMMEDIATE PRACTICE

A **Fill in the blanks with the appropriate forms of the words given.**

1. His behavior is _____ (bad) than ever before.

2. He is _____ (strong) than I expected.

3. It was _____ (expensive) than I thought.

4. He considered her opinion _____ (valuable) among ours.

5. This is _____ (good) beer that I have ever drunk.

6. He is _____ (suitable) person among us.

7. I had seen the film only a few days _____ (early).

8. I go there _____ (frequently) than she does.

9. He worked _____ (carefully) among the workers.

10. The horse ran _____ (fast) and came first in the race.

B Translate the following sentences into English.

1. 这是今年最严重的事故。

2. 我们要少花钱多办事。

3. 她的时间比我多。

4. 什么也不如在浴缸里发现虫子更令人不快。

5. 哪条河流是中国最长的？

6. 她决心以后更用功一些。

7. 你讲英语比其他人流利。

8. 谁到得最早？

9. 她表现得最大方。

10. 她唱歌像夜莺一样甜美。

PART III　TOWARD PRODUCTIVE LANGUAGE

READING ACTIVITIES

Read the following very quickly and try to get the general meaning; do not worry if you come across some new words.

> 蹦级、攀岩、悬崖跳水、空中冲浪……这些极限运动你熟悉吗？极限运动以它的新鲜、刺激逐渐成为时尚运动的代名词，越来越受到年轻人的欢迎。本篇课文为我们描述了许多极限运动，告诉我们极限运动流行的原因及其特征。通过阅读课文，你也来体验一下极限运动的快乐与刺激吧！

Text B

Extreme Sports

An extreme sport (also called action sport, adventure sport, and adventurous sport) is any sport or physical activity with a very high level of danger and often involves speed, height, and high level of physical exertion, highly specialized gear or spectacular stunts.

In the past, young athletes would play hockey or baseball. Today, they want risk and excitement—the closer to the edge the better. They snowboard over cliffs and mountain-bike down steep mountains. They wind-surf near hurricanes, go white-water rafting through rapids, and bungy-jump from towers.

Extreme sports started as an alternative to more expensive sports. A city kid who didn't have the money to buy expensive sports equipment could get a skateboard and have fun. But now it has become a whole

extreme /ɪkˈstriːm/ *adj.* 极度的，极端的；过激的
exertion /ɪɡˈzɜːʃən/ *n.* 用力，努力，费力
specialized /ˈspeʃəlaɪzd/ *adj.* 专门的，专科的
gear /ɡɪə/ *n.* 用具；设备；衣服
stunt /stʌnt/ *n.* 惊人的表演，特技，绝技
steep /stiːp/ *adj.* 陡的，急剧升降的
wind-surf /ˈwɪndsɜːf/ *v.* 风帆冲浪
white-water rafting 激流泛舟
rapids /ˈræpɪdz/ *n.* 激流，湍流
bungy-jump *n.* 蹦极
alternative /ɔːlˈtɜːnətɪv/ *n.* 两者择一，供替代的选择
skateboard /ˈskeɪtbɔːd/ *n.* 滑板

new area of sports, with specialized equipment and high levels of skill. There's even a special

15 Olympics for extreme sports, called the Winter X-games, which includes snow-mountain biking and

ice climbing.

What makes extreme sports so popular? "People love the thrill," says Murray Nussbaum, who

sells sports equipment. "City people want to be out-doors on the weekend and do something

challenging. The new equipment is so much better that people can take more risks without getting

20 hurt." An athlete adds, "Sure there's a risk, but that's part of the appeal. Once you go mountain

biking or snowboarding, it's impossible to go back to bike riding or skiing. It's just too boring."

An Extreme Games competition is held each summer in Rhode Island. It features sports such

as sky surfing, where people jump from air-planes with surfboards attached to their feet.

Rick Stevenson, 16 years old, spends every minute he can on the mountains. He and his friends

25 go snow-boarding every weekend. "It's incredible," he says. "The winds are so strong. The boards

go 50 miles an hour." His friend Laura Fields agrees. "No one goes skiing anymore," she says,

"that's for the old folks."

Last month 80 competitors from 10 nations went to Germany for the first world championship

of Extreme Ironing, a hot new board sport that combines the buzz of surfing with the satisfaction of

30 a well-pressed shirt. Challenged to let off steam in dangerous settings—from mountain peaks to

rapids—contestants were judged on the difficulty of their athletic undertaking and the quality of the

creases in their clothing.

These are of a new trend in sports. It has its own language, words such as "rage," "juice," and

"energy." It has its own clothing, such as skin-tight bicycle suits in rainbow colors or baggy tops

35 and pants. And it's not for the old or the easily frightened. Its philosophy is to get as close to the

edge as possible. And more and more young athletes

are taking part in these risky, daredevil activities

called "extreme sports," or "X-sports."

A feature of such activities in the view of some is

40 their capacity to induce an energy in participants.

Furthermore, a recent study suggests that the link to

thrill /θrɪl/ *n.* 强烈的兴奋、恐惧或快乐感
appeal /ə'piːl/ *n.* 感染力，吸引力；呼吁，恳求
sky surfing 空中冲浪滑翔（指在打开降落伞前踩着小冲浪板乘风翱翔的一种特技跳伞）
contestant /kən'testənt/ *n.* 竞争者；参赛者
baggy /'bægɪ/ *adj.* 宽松下垂的
philosophy /fɪ'lɒsəfɪ/ *n.* 哲学
daredevil /'deədevəl/ *adj.* 鲁莽大胆的

energy and "true" extreme sports is tentative. The study

defined "true" extreme sports as a leisure or recreation

activity where the most likely outcome of a mismanaged

45 accident or mistake was death. This definition was

designed to separate the marketing hype from the activity.   Another characteristic of such activities

is they tend to be individual rather than team sports.   Extreme sports can include both competitive

and non-competitive activities.

   Extreme sports are certainly not for everyone.   Most people still prefer to play baseball or

50 basketball or watch sports on TV.   But extreme sports are definitely gaining in popularity.   "These

sports are fresh and exciting. It's the wave of the future. The potential is huge," says Nussbaum.

| tentative /'tentətɪv/ *adj.* 试探性的，试验的，尝试性的 |
| recreation /rekrɪ'eɪʃən/ *n.* 娱乐(方式)，消遣(方式) |
| hype /haɪp/ *n.* 天花乱坠的广告宣传 |

READING COMPREHENSION

A **Choose the best answers for the following questions.**

1. The name of the Special Olympics for extreme sports is _____.

   A. Snow-mountain Biking   B. Winter X-games

   C. Extreme Sports   D. Ice Climbing

2. Why are extreme sports so popular? _____

   A. Because people want to do something challenging and exciting.

   B. Because they are fashionable.

   C. Because the extreme sports equipment is cheap.

   D. Because they are competitive.

3. Which of the following is NOT mentioned as extreme sports? _____

   A. Sky surfing.   B. Snow-boarding.

   C. Extreme ironing.   D. Hockey.

4. What is the philosophy of extreme sports? _____

    A. To have fun.

    B. To be the winner.

    C. To get as close to the edge as possible.

    D. To have its own language.

5. Which of the following is NOT true according to the passage? _____

    A. Extreme sports started as an alternative to more expensive sports.

    B. Extreme sports have their own language such as "energy" and "juice."

    C. A feature of extreme sports is their capacity to induce energy in participants.

    D. Extreme sports are competitive.

B Answer the following questions.

1. What is an extreme sport?

2. Why are extreme sports so popular?

3. What is sky surfing?

4. What kinds of people like extreme sports?

5. What are the features of extreme sports?

Unit 2

PART I PREPARATORY

WORDS IN CONTEXT

Read aloud the following sentences, paying attention to the meaning of the words in italics.

1. After the rain, the sun *emerged* from behind the clouds.

2. We offer a *personal* service to our customers.

3. The task is hard, however, we are determined to *fulfill* it.

4. Have you ever thought about becoming a *professional* musician?

5. Beware of him who regards not his *reputation*.

6. Boys have a stronger *tendency* to fight than girls.

7. The Chinese government actively supports and aids *financially* scientific studies.

8. For college students to do a part-time job will *broaden* their outlook.

9. The first walk on the moon is quite an *accomplishment*.

10. Hard work always takes your mind off *domestic* problems.

WORDS LEARNED IN DISPLAY

Write the meaning of each of the following words in the corresponding blank.   You can write either in English or in Chinese.

reputation _____

accomplishment _____

tendency _____

fulfill _____

financially _____

domestic _____

emerge _____

personal _____

professional _____

domestic _____

EXPRESSIONS IN CONTEXT

Study the following expressions and see how they are used in sentences.

in a sense 从某种意义上说

◇ In a sense, your personality lies in your sense of humor.

step into 进入

◇ Once you step into that company, you will become an office alcoholic.

apart from 除了

◇ Apart from a slight error, the answer is correct.

concentrate on 致力于;专心于

◇ We must concentrate our efforts on improving education.

due to 由于

◇ All the buses are late due to heavy traffic.

be renowned for 以……闻名

◇ Suzhou is renowned to the world for its arts and crafts.

acquaint oneself with 使熟悉，了解，知道

◇ You must acquaint yourself with your new duties.

last but not least 最后但并不是最不重要的

◇ Last but not least, you should prepare for the coming exam.

EXPRESSIONS LEARNED IN DISPLAY

Complete each of the following sentences with the expressions you have just learned.

1. Manufacturing firms in Hong Kong _____ their products.

2. Please _____ the facts of the case, I am in need of every detail.

3. _____ the heavy snow, the railroad was blocked.

4. A driver should _____ the road when driving.

5. _____ your duties, you have to fulfill your task successfully.

6. _____, your answer is better than the key in the reference book.

7. He put forward several pieces of advice to protect the nature. _____, to awake people's consciousness is the best choice.

8. The manager _____ his office angrily for he lost an important chance.

PART II LANGUAGE IN CONTEXT

Read the following summary in Chinese and think what you are going to read in this text.

收藏艺术珍品是大家的梦想,但是专家呼吁"艺术品交易会不是超市"。中国的艺术品交易会起步晚但发展较快,一些交易会通过吸引投资、出售艺术品等方式已经获得经济独立。出售艺术品不是交易会的唯一目的,因为艺术品的价值不仅在于价格,更在于格调、鉴赏性和社会意义。艺术品陶冶了人们的情操,而交易会则给中外文化提供了交流平台,促进了某些地域的经济发展,成为文化产业的重要组成部分。

PREVIEW QUESTIONS

Work in pairs or groups and discuss the following questions.

1. What is an art fair?

2. Do people hold art fairs only to sell art works like in the supermarkets?

3. When and where did China step into art fairs?

4. Can you list some ways to gather financial support for air fairs?

5. What is the importance of art fairs?

6. Who may benefit from art fairs?

READING SELECTION

Text A

Art Fairs Are Not Supermarkets

It is a dream for many people to collect rare treasure. In recent years, along with rapid economic development, the art market is also rising, and various kinds of art fairs have quickly emerged, together with a too high, too hot and too fast market.

Amid such a climate some experts have angrily pointed out that, "Art fairs are not

5　supermarkets!" An art work can fulfill its commercial value in the market, but it is not the only value of the art.

China began its step into the world of art fairs quite late. In 1993, the first China Art Exposition was held by the Ministry of China Culture in Guangzhou, which developed into the most famous official fair of the country. The standardized art galleries in China then could be

10　counted on just one hand.

Early art fairs were almost personal exhibitions for trade, just like supermarkets of art for selling, which were not real modern art fairs in a strict sense, let alone when compared with world famous art fairs, such as Basel Art Fair.

In recent years, the art market in China has grown by leaps and bounds and galleries gradu-

15　ally expanded so that professional modern art fairs came into being. Today art fairs in China have a good tendency for specialization and internationaliza- tion, and many exhibition brands have earned world wide reputations.

20　However, in such a hot art market, is it high prices or cool-headed academic thinking that leads the trend? What is it that influences the taste and style of the art fair? If the art fair concentrates on the sale

treasure /ˈtreʒə/ *n.* 珍宝
art fairs 艺术展览会
emerge /ɪˈmɜːdʒ/ *vi.* 出现, 显出
fulfill /fʊlˈfɪl/ *vt.* 实现, 履行
step into 涉足
official /əˈfɪʃəl/ *adj.* 官方的
personal /ˈpɜːsənəl/ *adj.* 个人的
in a strict sense 严格说来
professional /prəˈfeʃənəl/ *adj.* 专业的
come into being 开始存在
tendency /ˈtendənsi/ *n.* 倾向, 趋势
reputation /ˌrepjʊˈteɪʃən/ *n.* 声誉
influence /ˈɪnflʊəns/ *vt.* 影响
concentrate on 将……集中于……

price and total revenue, it will inevitably lead to the situation where "to sell what is hot."

Due to the current Chinese economy as being in "the primary stage of socialism," art fairs are now and will continue to be dual-track. Government leading art fairs are partly invested by the government, while commercial art fairs are totally dependent on self owned capital or social capital, and manage their own business, so they must achieve economic benefit to develop. Thus art fairs firstly have to attract investment at full capacity, and that is why the overall level of art works in an art fair is not high and uneven.

In the next place, commercial art fairs must do their best to sell art works. The most famous Basel Art Fair is renowned for its high turnover and the number of art works featured. The manager of Basel Art Fair said that the measure of a successful art fair is how many paintings are sold. Though inelegant, it is true, because one art galley has to pay 100 thousand Swiss francs to exhibit their paintings in the Basel Art Fair. In this sense, no matter how strong the art gallery is, it can not survive without financial income in art fairs.

However, to judge an art fair's success or failure only from economic benefit is not enough. Apart from market value pervaded by artists' creation, there are also many social benefits of art fairs.

Unlike residents in western developed countries who often go to museums and art exhibitions to broaden their knowledge and artistic accomplishment, Chinese are weak on aesthetics and art education. As such various art fairs that gather outstanding art work home or abroad, offer common residents in China a chance to learn schools of all kinds of styles, and to appreciate famous works from splendid artists.

Art fairs are a platform for cultural exchange between Chinese and foreign art institutions. By face to face communication, Chinese art galleries can learn operating experience to lift the level of the whole art market. Besides, it is also a good

due to 由于
dual-track 双轨的
dependent /dɪ'pendənt/ *adj.* 依靠的，依赖的
investment /ɪn'vestmənt/ *n.* 投资
be renowned for 以……著称
measure /'meʒə/ *n.* 量度，测量
inelegant /ɪn'elɪgənt/ *adj.* 不雅的，粗俗的
survive /sə'vaɪv/ *vi.* 生存，存活
financial /faɪ'nænʃəl/ *adj.* 经济上的，财政的
apart from 除了
resident /'rezɪdənt/ *n.* 居民
broaden /'brɔːdn/ *vt.* 拓宽
accomplishment /ə'kʌmplɪʃmənt/ *n.* 成就
outstanding /ˌaʊt'stændɪŋ/ *adj.* 出众的
appreciate /ə'priːʃɪeɪt/ *vt.* 欣赏
communication /kəˌmjuːnɪ'keɪʃən/ *n.* 交流

chance to get domestic and foreign businessmen to participate in art fairs and for them to acquaint themselves with the overall situation of Chinese artists.

domestic /dəˈmestɪk/ **adj.** 国内的；家庭的；家养的
acquaint oneself with 让……知道，了解
regional /ˈriːdʒənəl/ **adj.** 地区的

55   Last but not least, art fairs have regional comprehensive benefits. Basel once was a small town in Switzerland, though now has benefited greatly from this. Every year 40 billon Euro is traded, and hundreds of thousands of people rush to fill up hotels in cities and towns around. During recent years, art fairs in big cities such as Beijing and Shanghai have also begun to show great regional comprehensive benefits with the increasing scale, attracting
60 great attention from the government.

Art fairs should be seen as an important part of cultural industry and the exhibition economy, as a name card of the city while also showing the soft power of the region.

COMPREHENSION CHECK

Understanding the General Ideas

Discuss the following questions in pairs or groups. The key words given in the brackets may help you in your discussion.

1. How is the development of art fairs ?

   (rising, emerge, too high, too hot and too fast)

2. In what ways does a modern art fair finance itself?

   (dual-track, leading, partly invested by the government, financially independent)

3. How do art fairs benefit visitors?

   (broaden artistic accomplishment, learn artistic styles, appreciate outstanding artworks)

4. What effects can art fairs bring to the region where they are located?

   (market, attract attention from the government, regional economy)

5. What values of art fairs are mentioned in the passage?

(commercial, artistic benefits, social benefits, communication, cultural exchange)

Understanding the Specifics

Read the following sentences and tell if they are true or false according to the text. In the brackets leading each statement, put "T" for true or "F" for false.

1. (　　) The only reason why people open up art fairs is to make money.

2. (　　) Experts are angry about the fact that modern art fairs are like supermarkets.

3. (　　) The first China Art Exposition was held in Guangzhou in 1993.

4. (　　) Professional art fairs appear in China for the government invested a large sum of money.

5. (　　) Art fairs are a platform for cultural exchange between art institutions.

6. (　　) No matter how strong an art fair is, it can not survive without income.

7. (　　) Basel, a town in Netherlands, has financially benefited from art fairs.

8. (　　) Though art fairs bring financial benefits, they can't bring any reputation to the region.

STUDY AND PRACTICE

Vocabulary

Fill in the blanks with the words below. Change the form where necessary.

emerge	personal	fulfill	professional
reputation	tendency	financially	broaden
accomplishment	domestic		

1. Will you mind answering a few _____ questions?

2. You should _____ your experience by traveling more.

3. The first walk on the moon is quite an _____ .

4. At present, 8,000 orphans are _____ supported in their school education.

5. Alice made her decision to be a _____ model.

6. The rabbit will not _____ from its hole while you are there.

7. Old citizens always have a _____ to forget things.

8. It is the female who does the _____ affairs every day in many cultures.

9. This store has an excellent _____ for fair dealing.

10. A nurse has to _____ many duties in caring for the sick.

Expressions

Rewrite the following sentences with help of the phrases and expressions provided. The italicized part in each sentence may serve as the hints for your task. The first sentence is done for you.

in a sense	be renowned for	apart from
concentrate on	due to	step into
acquaint oneself with	last but not least	

1. You are right *to some degree*, but you don't know all the facts.

   You are right in a sense, but you don't know all the facts.

2. After graduation John *started* his career as a lawyer.

   _____

3. *Except for* some spelling mistakes, the composition is fairly good.

   _____

4. We must *focus* our efforts *on* finding ways to reduce costs.

5. The chairman's absence is *caused by* illness.

6. He *was famous for* his contribution to psychology.

7. He *got to know about* every aspect of the question.

8. *Last and also the most important,* the bride arrived on the wedding ceremony.

Translation

A From Chinese to English

1. 请告知贵方的艺术博览会计划。

2. 它将推动中国文化与世界其他文化的广泛交流。

3. 我来告诉你这件事的真相。

4. 我们决定一心一意搞建设是正确的。

5. 显示屏将会播放国内外重要新闻。

6. 他在这个镇上是很有权势的人。

7. 应该鼓励孩子独立思考。

8. 她走进屋子在沙发上坐下。

B From English to Chinese

1. An art work can fulfill its commercial value in the market, but it is not the only value of the art.

2. In recent years, the art market in China has grown quickly and galleries expanded so that professional art fairs came into being.

3. Due to the current economy , art fairs are now and will continue to be dual-track.

4. No matter how strong the art gallery is, it can not survive without income.

5. Besides, it is a good chance to get domestic and foreign businessmen to participate in art fairs and acquaint themselves with more artists.

GRAMMAR

Commparative Degrees of Adjectives and Adverbs
(形容词和副词的比较级) (II)

1. 比较级的用法

和 than 一起用,表示两者相比,也可以不用 than:

Skiing is more exciting than skating.

He is stronger than I expected.

It's better to be prepared than unprepared.

She was more surprised than angry.

Try to do better next time.

2. 比较级的修饰语

比较级前可加 much, a lot, a little, any, no 以及数词等:

You have far more imagination than I have.

Do you feel any better today?

She is no older than Zilla.

Cotton output was 20 per cent higher than in the previous year.

She could dance even more gracefully than a dancer.

3. 比较级的特殊用法

1）"more... than"有时可以把两种品质加以比较, 表示"更多……而不是"：

I was more annoyed than worried when he didn't come home.

This is more a war movie than a historical film.

2）more and more 这类结构可表示"越来越"：

The story gets more and more exciting.

It rained more and more heavily.

3）the more... the more 可表示"越是……越……"：

The more learned a man is, the more modest he usually is.

The more difficult the questions are, the less likely I am to be able to answer them.

4）less than 常表示"不到……"或"不太"：

I bought it for less than a dollar.

The boys were less than happy about having a party.

5）more than 常用在数词前, 表示"超过……"、"……多"：

He can't be more than thirty.

More than 800 people attended the concert.

6）no less than 表示"多达"、"不少于"：

He won no less than $ 500.

Its population is no less than two million.

7）more or less 表示"基本上"、"大体上"或"大约"：

The work is more or less finished.

The answer was more or less right.

4. as...as 和 not as (so)...as 结构

1) as 可表示"和……一样……":

Some of their states are as big as France.

I can jump as high as Bill.

She can read twice as fast as he does.

2) 在否定句中可用 not as...或 not so...表示"不像……那样":

The food wasn't as good as yesterday.

I don't go there as much as I used to.

Your coffee is not as (so) good as the coffee my mother makes.

He is not so handsome as his brother.

3) 在 as...as 结构中也可以插入修饰语:

Petrol is twice as expensive as it was a few years ago.

My command of English is not half so (as) good as yours.

5. 最高级的用法

1) 形容词最高级主要表示"最……",前面一般带定冠词 the; 副词最高级可修饰动词,前面有时可不带定冠词 the:

It was the quickest route from Rome to Milan.

I shall give a prize to the pupil who reads best.

Of the four of us, I sang (the) worst.

2) 形容词最高级前面有时可有一个状语或定语修饰:

It was by far the best hospital I had ever seen.

Hainan is China's second largest island.

A **Fill in the blanks with the appropriate forms of the words given.**

1. Holiday flights are getting _____ (expensive) and students can afford to go traveling on holidays.

2. Your English is getting _____ (good).

3. We were busy and _____ (delighted) to have company that day.

4. He is _____ (energetic) a young man.

5. She was at her _____ (happy) in the presence of her mother.

6. We were all _____ (anxious) to go home.

7. Cotton output was 20 per cent _____ (high) than in the previous year.

8. He is _____ (much) than a friend to me.

9. Manchester is _____ (far) from London than Oxford is.

10. He didn't have _____ (little) desire to go to bed.

B **Translate the following sentences into English.**

1. 坐飞机到那里比坐火车快。

2. 他是运气好，而不是聪明。

3. 她的实际年龄比她看上去要大得多。

4. 它比市场价格低四分之一。

5. 对他们来说，音乐是一种生活方式而不仅仅是一种爱好。

6. 从这里到火车站大约有一英里。

7. 你应当懂得这样冷的天不穿大衣出去可不行。

8. 他本想和我顶嘴的，但没有这样做。

9. 我讲得不及你一半好。

10. 改天我们再多聊聊。

READING ACTIVITIES

Read the following very quickly and try to get the general meaning; do not worry if you come across some new words.

> 龙在中国文化中意味深远,中国人民自称"龙的传人"。舞龙作为中国传统艺术中极具代表性的表演方式,不仅具有收获、祈福等意义,在现代也被赋予了新的历史意义——团队协作精神。文章介绍了舞龙表演中"龙"的组成部分,介绍了手脚合作和团员合作的重要性,其推广受到了国内外人民的欢迎。

Text B

Dragon Dance

Dragons are deeply rooted in the Chinese culture.   People showed great respect for dragons, which could be found in pictures and writings.   As a result the dragon has become the symbol of Chinese nation. The Chinese often consider themselves as the descendants of the dragon.

Some myths are about the dragon. Over a century ago, inhabitants of Tai Hang lived by farming
5 and fishing. A few days before the Mid-Autumn Festival, a typhoon attacked the village. While the villagers were repairing the damage, a huge snake came and ate domestic animals. It was said that the snake was the son of the Dragon King.   The only way to stop it was to dance a fire dance for three days during the Mid-Autumn Festival.   So the villagers made a big fire dragon of straw and lit firecrackers. In the end, the disaster disappeared. From then on, the dragon dance became a special
10 performance of arts in the Chinese activities and spread throughout China and to the whole world.

According to ancient history, the dragon dance was also taught in schools to provide more courage.   Now

symbol /'sɪmbəl/ *n.* 象征,标志
descendant /dɪ'sendənt/ *n.* 后代,后裔
typhoon /taɪ'fuːn/ *n.* 台风

the meaning of the dragon dance has changed a lot. Besides belief and respect towards the dragon, it also symbolizes good luck and prosperity in the year to come for all the human beings.

15   A dragon includes a pearl, the head, the body and the tail. The length depends on the human power, financial power, materials, skills and size of the field. A small organization cannot afford to run a very long dragon because it consumes great human power, expenses and special skills. The normal length and size of the dragon body is 112 feet and is divided into 9 major sections. The distance of each minor (rib-like) section is 14 inches apart , therefore the body has 81 rings.

20   To make a successful dance, the combination and timing of the different parts of the dragon are very important. Any mistakes made by any performers of the dragon dance team would spoil the whole performance. The pearl of the dragon must be able to cooperate with the body of the dragon. Thus, the pearl holder must have high skill to time with the beat of the drum.

     The dragon head weights 12 kilos and the performer must be energetic. The tail also has to
25 keep in time with head movements. The fourth and fifth sections are considered to be the middle portion and the performers must be very alert as the body movement changes from time to time.

     The patterns of the dragon dance are changed according to the skills and experiences acquired by the performers. To perform an outstanding dragon dance, performers must be able to run in the correct steps, neither too quick nor too slow. The team members should be able to leap and crouch
30 at the same time when needed. Their steps should change with the different positions of the hands as the movements of the dance depend very much on the hands. Sometimes one should uphold the part in hand while sometimes one should put it as low as possible. All the successful movements depend on the cooperation of the whole team and
35 strict discipline. Every performer must play his role well in good timing and combination with other members.

     History tells us that the dragon dance is performed in various ways, types and colors. Green
40 is the main color of the dragon which sym-

symbolize /'sɪmbəlaɪz/ vt. 象征;作为……的象征
depend on 依赖,依靠
organization /,ɔːgənaɪ'zeɪʃən/ n. 组织,机构,团体
consume /kən'sjuːm/ vt. 消耗,消费,耗尽
section /'sekʃən/ n. 部分
combination /,kɒmbɪ'neɪʃən/ n. 结合,组合
timing /'taɪmɪŋ/ n. 时机
energetic /,enə'dʒetɪk/ adj. 精力充沛的,充满活力的
portion /'pɔːʃən/ n. 一部分,一份
leap /liːp/ vi. 跳,跳跃
crouch /kraʊtʃ/ vi. 屈膝,蹲伏

bolizes a great harvest. Yellow symbolizes the solemn empire, golden prosperity, red excitement while its scales and tail are mostly beautiful silver, glittering at all times and providing a joyous atmosphere. As the

45 dragon dance is not performed everyday, the cloth of the dragon is to be removed and repainted before the next performance.

empire /'empaɪə/ *n.* 帝国
scale /skeɪl/ *n.* 鳞，鳞片
joyous /'dʒɔɪəs/ *adj.* 快乐的，使人喜悦的
atmosphere /'ætməsfɪə/ *n.* 气氛，环境
remove /rɪ'muːv/ *vt.* 移走；排除
significance /sɪg'nɪfɪkəns/ *n.* 重大意义，重要性

Now the dragon dance is not only a ceremony, but also a popular activity. People celebrate a festival or a special time by dancing a dragon dance. The ancient pattern has new significance — teamwork spirit of the Chinese.

READING COMPREHENSION

A Choose the best answers for the following questions.

1. In Chinese eyes, dragons are sacred because _____ .

    A. dragons are imaginary animals

    B. the Chinese created dragons

    C. the Chinese consider themselves as the descendants of the dragon

    D. the Chinese suffered the disasters brought by dragons

2. According to the myth in the passage, the only way to stop a fierce dragon was to _____ .

    A. dance a fire dance for three days

    B. kill it while it is sleeping

    C. set fire to the dragon

    D. beg the Dragon King to take its son home

3. Which section is not a part of a dragon dance?

    A. The pearl.   B. The canvas.   C. The body.   D. The tail.

4. Which of the following sentence is correct according to the passage?

    A. Performers must be able to run in the correct steps as quickly as possible.

    B. A very long dragon may not consume great human power, expenses and special skills if operated properly.

    C. To make a successful dance, the combination and timing of the different parts of the dragon are very important.

    D. The cloth of the dragon is to be removed and repainted before the next performance to show respect.

5. _____ is the new significance given to dragon dance in contemporary times.

    A. Prosperity   B. Great harvest

    C. Joyous atmosphere   D. Teamwork spirit of the Chinese

B **Answer the following questions.**

1. What does the concept dragon mean in the Chinese culture?

2. How has the dragon dance come into being?

3. What does a dragon consist of in the dragon dance?

4. What do the colors on the dragon symbolize?

5. Is there any new significance of the dragon dance? What is it?

Unit 3

PART I   PREPARATORY

Read aloud the following sentences, paying attention to the meaning of the words in italics.

1. He attended the ceremony as a *distinguished* guest.

2. A great wave *overwhelmed* the boat.

3. Elizabeth thought he was an *arrogant* and selfish man.

4. The children all have very different *personalities*.

5. This is the *inevitable* course of history.

6. Prejudice sometimes *hampers* a person from doing the right thing.

7. He could not control his *passion*.

8. The country was *humiliated* by defeat.

9. He achieved great *triumphs*.

10. I *conquered* my dislike for mathematics.

Write the meaning of each of the following words in the corresponding blank. You can write either in English or in Chinese.

distinguished _____

overwhelm _____

arrogant _____

personality _____

inevitable _____

hamper _____

passion _____

humiliate _____

triumph _____

conquer _____

EXPRESSIONS IN CONTEXT

Study the following expressions and see how they are used in sentences.

gain from 从……获得

◇ Many voters feel that the country would gain from a change of leadership.

above all 首先; 尤其是

◇ He was above all a good and tireless writer.

dream of 做梦(梦见)

◇ I often dreamed of my parents soon after I left home.

make a mess (of) (把……)弄糟(搞坏);(把……)搞得一塌糊涂

◇ This illness makes a mess of my holiday plans.

care about 在乎,在意

◇ They don't care about the expenses.

some sort of 某种的;仿佛;多少有些

◇ There's some sort of sticky fluid on the kitchen floor.

knock out 粗略地(匆匆地)创作(完成);使筋疲力尽

◇ He knocked out five letters in two hours last night.

take ... seriously 认真对待,严肃对待

◇ He never takes anything seriously

EXPRESSIONS LEARNED IN DISPLAY

Complete each of the following sentences with the expressions you have just learned.

1. When I lived with my father, I _____ much knowledge _____ him.

2. I never _____ such a thing.

3. But _____ tell me quickly what I have to do.

4. This job has quite _____ me _____ .

5. I don't _____ much _____ music.

6. He _____ his work.

7. He could not _____ such questions _____ .

8. Don't worry about price—I'm sure we can come to _____ arrangement.

PART II LANGUAGE IN CONTEXT

Read the following summary in Chinese and think what you are going to read in this text.

老一辈人希望年轻人懂得什么?他们想与年轻人分享什么样的人生经验?著名摄影家安德鲁·萨克曼采访了全球50位65岁以上的名人,他们的人生感悟值得我们体味和学习。本文挑选了其中的6位。

PREVIEW QUESTIONS

Work in pairs or groups and discuss the following questions.

1. When you were a child, did you dream of doing anything important or special in the future?

2. What do you usually do to protect the environment?

3. In order to succeed in one's profession, what do you think are the most fundamental?

READING SELECTION

Text A

Six Celebrities Share What They've Learned

celebrity /sɪˈlebrɪti/ *n.* (尤指娱乐界的) 名人,名流

What is the greatest gift from one generation to

generation /ˌdʒenəˈreɪʃən/ *n.* 一代人,一代

40

the next? It's wisdom gained from experience. The photographer Andrew Zuckerman traveled to seven countries, flew 65,000 miles, and drove 5,000 more, in order to ask 50 distinguished individuals aged 65 years and older what they would like others to know. The following is a
5 selection.

DESMOND TUTU—cleric; winner, 1984 Nobel Peace Prize; winner, 2005 Gandhi Peace Prize

"Each one of us can make a contribution. Too frequently we think we have to do spectacular things. Yet if we remember that the sea is actually made up of drops of water and each drop is
10 important, each one of us can do our little bit where we are. Those little bits can come together and almost overwhelm the world. Each one of us can be an oasis of peace."

JANE GOODALL—primatologist and
15 conservationist

"We've been very arrogant in assuming that there's a sharp line dividing us from the rest of the animal kingdom. We are not the only beings on this planet with personalities,
20 minds, and, above all, emotions. We need to be more respectful.

wisdom /'wɪzdəm/ *n.* 智慧，知识，学问
gain from 从……获得
distinguished /dɪ'stɪŋgwɪʃt/ *adj.* 卓越的；著名的；受人尊敬的
cleric /'klerɪk/ *n.* 牧师，教士，神职人员
contribution /ˌkɒntrɪ'bjuːʃ ə n/ *n.* 捐助物；贡献
spectacular /spek'tækjʊlə/ *adj.* 引人注目的；轰动一时的；惊人的
overwhelm /ˌəʊvə'welm/ *vt.* 淹没；制服；压倒
oasis /əʊ'eɪsɪs/ *n.* 绿洲
primatologist /ˌpraɪmə'tɒlədʒɪst/ *n.* 灵长类行为学家
conservationist /ˌkɒnsə'veɪʃ ə nɪst/ *n.* 自然资源保护者，生态环境保护者
arrogant /'ærəgənt/ *adj.* 傲慢的，自大的
personality /ˌpɜːsə'næləti/ *n.* 人格，个性
above all 首先，尤其是

41

As a child, I dreamed of going to Africa, living there with the animals. Such an amazing thing happened. Being out on my own in nature, with or without the chimpanzees, is just

25 something I loved.

The most important thing we can do to try to get out of the mess we've made on this planet is to spend time thinking about the consequences of the choices we make. What did we eat? How was it grown? Did it adversely affect animals? Is it good for human health? What do we wear? Where was it made?

30 Could we make it in a way that is less damaging to the environment? If we start thinking like that, inevitably people make small changes. And if people start making small changes, then we start getting the major change that we must have if we care about the future for our children."

CLINT EASTWOOD—actor, more than 50 films; director, 29 films, including *Unforgiven* (《不可饶恕》)and *Million Dollar Baby* (《百万美元宝贝》); winner, 4 Academy Awards

35 "Great stories teach you something. That's one reason I haven't slipped into some sort of retirement: I always feel like I'm learning something new.

There was a time in my life when I was doing westerns, on the plains of Spain. I could have stayed there and probably knocked out a dozen more. But the time came when I said 'That's enough of that.' As fun as they were to do, it was time to move on. If a story doesn't

40 have anything that's fresh in it, at least for me, I move away from it.

Take your profession seriously; don't take yourself seriously. If you take yourself seriously, you're not going to be able to move forward. You're going to be

45 hampered by always wanting to look in the mirror and see if you have enough tuna oil on your hair or something like that."

LELLA and MASSIMO VIGNELLI—interior

dream of 做梦(梦见)
mess /mes/ *n.* 杂乱,脏乱
make a mess (of) (把……)弄糟[搞坏];
(把……)搞得一塌糊涂
consequence /'kɒnsɪkwəns/ *n.* 结果,后果
adversely /'ædvɜːsli/ *adv.* 不利地,有害地
care about 在乎,在意
western /'westən/ *n.* 西部片,西部小说
some sort of 某种;仿佛;多少有些
knock out 使筋疲力尽;使竭尽全力;粗略
地[匆匆地]创作[完成]
take ... seriously 认真对待,严肃对待
hamper /'hæmpə/ *vt.* 妨碍,束缚,限制
tuna /'tjuːnə/ *n.* 金枪鱼

42

and graphic design team, married 50 years; winners, more than 130 awards

50　LV: "People ask us, 'Aren't you retiring?' But we really like what we do."

MV: "You need to have passion. The greatest thing I've learned in my life is that there is room for everybody.　That's the great thing about art and design and communication.　There's room for all."

LV: "Aspiring designers should know about the good things that happened before. Have a
55　little history. Go back and see what was done before."

MV: "Learn from the past if you want what matters in the present. Knowledge is the most important thing. To young people, we say, 'Fill your brain with as much information as you can. Look at everything, know everything, develop a critical mind. History, theory, and criticism are the three fundamental elements to grow in a professional life.　History will provide you with the
60　tools for understanding. Theory will be the philosophy of why you're doing it. And criticism will provide you with the ability to continually master what you are doing.　Play with these tools and you can do pretty good things.' "

NELSON MANDELA—civil rights leader; prisoner for 27 years for his antiapartheid work; cowinner, 1993
65　Nobel Peace Prize;　elected South Africa's first freely chosen president (1994—1999)

"Wounds that can't be seen are more painful than those that can be seen and cured by a doctor.　I learned that to humiliate another person is to make him suffer
70　an unnecessarily cruel fate.　I learned that courage was

passion /'pæʃən/ **n.** 激情，热情
aspiring /əs'paɪərɪŋ/ **adj.** 有追求的
critical /'krɪtɪkəl/ **adj.** 决定性的，关键性的；危急的；批评的，批判的
fundamental /ˌfʌndə'mentl/ **adj.** 基本的；重要的；必要的
antiapartheid /'æntiə'pɑːtheɪt/ **adj.** 反种族隔离的
humiliate /hju'mɪlieɪt/ **vt.** 使蒙羞，羞辱，使丢脸

not the absence of fear but the triumph over it. I felt fear myself more times than I can remember, but I hid it behind a mask of boldness. The brave man is not he who does not feel afraid but he who conquers fear.

75 Where people of goodwill get together and transcend their differences for the common good, peaceful and just solutions can be found, even for those problems that seem most intractable."

triumph /'traɪəmf/ *n.* 胜利，成功
mask /mɑːsk/ *n.* 口罩；面具；掩饰
boldness /'bəʊldnɪs/ *n.* 大胆，冒失
conquer /'kɒŋkə/ *vt.* 攻克；征服；克服
goodwill /'gʊd'wɪl/ *n.* 善意，亲切，友好
transcend /træn'send/ *vt.* 超出，超越；胜过
common good 公益
intractable /ɪn'træktəbəl/ *adj.* 难对付的，难解决的

COMPREHENSION CHECK

Understanding the General Ideas

Discuss the following questions in pairs or groups. The key words given in the brackets may help you in your discussion.

1. How did Andrew Zuckerman acquire what others have learned?

   (traveled, distinguished, individuals)

2. Give a brief summary of Desmond Tutu's words.

   (contribution, peace)

3. What does Jane Goodall think of the most important thing we can do?

   (consequence, animals, the future)

4. How are you able to move forward according to the director of *Million Dollar Baby*?

   (take... seriously)

5. In Massimo Vignelli's opinion, what are the three fundamental elements to grow in a professional life, and why?

   (history; theory; criticism)

Understanding the Specifics

Read the following sentences and tell if they are true or false according to the text. In the brackets leading each statement, put "T" for true or "F" for false.

1. (   ) Andrew Zuckerman is 65 years old.

2. (   ) Desmond Tutu is the winner of 1984 Gandhi Peace Prize.

3. (   ) As a child, Jane Goodall dreamed of living in Africa with the animals.

4. (   ) Clint Eastwood directed *Unforgiven* and *Million Dollar Baby*.

5. (   ) Clint Eastwood did westerns on the plains of Spain in the past.

6. (   ) In Massimo Vignelli's life, the greatest thing he has learned is that there is room for everybody.

7. (   ) Nelson Mandela thought that courage was the absence of fear.

8. (   ) Nelson Mandela was a prisoner for 27 years for his antiapartheid work.

STUDY AND PRACTICE

Vocabulary

Fill in the blanks with the words below. Change the form where necessary.

overwhelm	conquer	individual	contribution
arrogant	consequence	adversely	hamper
triumph	celebrity		

1. Lots of _____ were at the film premiere.

2. The mountain was finally _____ by climbers in 1980.

45

3. The purpose of the law is to protect the right of the _____ .

4. I _____ a pound towards Jane's leaving present.

5. The act was adopted by a(n) _____ majority.

6. He has been very _____ .

7. Nobody can tell what the _____ may be.

8. Dirt and disease are _____ to the best growth of children.

9. Prejudice sometimes _____ a person from doing the right thing.

10. He had met the challenge and _____ .

Expressions

Rewrite the following sentences with help of the phrases and expressions provided. The italicized part in each sentence may serve as the hints for your task. The first sentence is done for you.

gain from	above all	dream of	care about
knock out	take seriously	provide with	not but

1. He thought he would *benefit from* going to school.

   He thought he would gain from going to school.

2. *First of all*, you should know what profession suits you.

   _____

3. She *dreamed about* a handsome young prince coming to rescue her from her misery.

   _____

4. I am really *fond of* the students in my class.

   _____

5. This job has quite *done me in*.

_____

6. They did *think much of* the plan.

_____

7. They *furnished* us *with* food.

_____

8. She is like a singer, *in fact*, she is a film star.

_____

Translation

A From Chinese to English

1. 我们希望从投资中获得收益。

2. 这份工作要求你要勤奋、有幽默感,但最重要的是要自信。

3. 近期内我不考虑出国读书。

4. 年轻人应该关心老人。

5. 那本书确实引起了我的共鸣。

6. 你的建议我总是认真对待的。

7. 供应给他们的食品不足。

8. 这所房子便是那位伟人出生的地方。

B From English to Chinese

1. Yet if we remember that the sea is actually made up of drops of water and each drop is important, each one of us can do our little bit where we are.

2. We are not the only beings on this planet with personalities, minds, and, above all, emotions.

3. And if people start making small changes, then we start getting the major change that we must have if we care about the future for our children.

4. Learn from the past if you want what matters in the present.

5. Wounds that can't be seen are more painful than those that can be seen and cured by a doctor.

GRAMMAR

Modal Auxiliaries (情态动词) (I)

1. 概述

情态动词与基本助动词的最主要区别之一是，基本助动词本身没有词汇意义，而情态动词则有自己的词汇意义，能表示说话者对所说话语的态度和看法，或者表示主观设想及其他情态意义。常见的情态动词有 can, could, may, might, will, would, need, dare, must, shall, should, ought to, used to 等。

2. 情态动词的意义和用法

1) can 的意义和用法

   (1) 表示能力(即能做某事)，通常是指由体力、知识、技能等产生的能力，如：

   Baby Tom can walk now.

   I can come to your party, but Alice can't. She's got to go to a meeting.

   (2) 表示许可，常见于口语，如：

   You can smoke in this room.

   Can I go for a swim this afternoon, Mum?

   (3) 表示可能，可用于肯定陈述句、否定句和疑问句，但更频繁地用于否定句和疑问句。

   Lightning can be dangerous.

We've got a map. We can't lose our way.

Can the news be true?

2) may 的意义和用法

(1) 表示许可，在肯定陈述句中，通常是指说话人给予的许可，如：

You may smoke in the room. (=You are permitted (by me) to...)

You may come if you wish.

在否定陈述句中，用 may not 表示说话人不许可，如：

You may not go. (=I do not permit you to...)

(2) 表示可能，通常只用于肯定陈述句或否定陈述句，如：

It may rain tomorrow. (=It is possible that...)

You may lose your way if you don't take a map.

He may be working in his study.

He may have been there.

I may have misunderstood you.

They may have been discussing the problem the whole day.

用 may 表示"可能"一般不用于疑问句，在疑问句中通常用 can 表示：

Can it be true?

What can he be thinking of?

(3) 用于表示祝福或诅咒，如：

May God bless you!

May you enjoy many years of health and happiness.

3）must 的意义和用法

(1) 表示必须，在肯定陈述句中，must 这一用法通常表示说话人的主观意志，或要求对方必须做某事，如：

I must go now, or I'll be late.

We must rely on the masses.

You must be here by ten o'clock.

must 表示"必须"，在疑问句中是征求听话人意见，是否必须做某事，如：

A: Must they go with you? (=Will you oblige them to go with you?)

B: Yes, they must. (=Yes, I do oblige them to go.)

在回答上述问题时, 如果是否定的答复, 不能用 mustn't, 而需要用 don't have to 或 needn't, 如:

A: Must you leave so soon?

B: No, I don't have to go yet. / No, I needn't.

must not 是表示说话人不许可或禁止某人做某事, 如:

You must not (mustn't) keep us all waiting. (=I oblige you not to keep us all waiting.)

You mustn't talk like that. (=I forbid you to talk like that.)

(2) 表示必然, 可以表示根据逻辑推理必然要发生某事, 如:

All men must die. (=All men will certainly die.)

Bad seeds must (=will certainly) bring bad crops.

(3) 表示推测, 指在说话人看来一定是、必然是, 一般也只用于肯定陈述句, 如:

It must be very late (=Probably it is very late) because the streets are quite deserted.

There must be a mistake.

He must be enjoying himself.

He must be feeling rather tired.

如果是推测过去时间发生的事情, 就用 must+ 不定式完成时或完成进行时, 如:

You must have left your handbag in the theatre.

Her eyes are red. She must have been crying.

当 must 用于推测意义时, 其否定形式通常不是 must not, 而是 cannot, 如:

If Fred didn't leave here before five, he can't be home yet.

He can't have been to your home. He doesn't know your address.

IMMEDIATE PRACTICE

Fill in the blanks with the modal auxiliaries you just learned.

1. Two eyes _____ (see) more than one.

2. You_____ (go) and see a doctor at once because you've got a fever.

3. —Can you speak Japanese?

   —No, I _____ .

4. —He _____ (be) in the classroom, I think.

   —No, he _____ (be) in the classroom. I saw him go home a minute ago.

5. _____ I take this one?

6. The children_____ (play) football on the road.

7. —Must I do my homework at once?

   —No, you _____ .

8. The room is in a terrible mess; it _____ (clean).

9. Passengers _____ (cross) by the footbridge.

10. There's a lot of noise from the next door. They _____ (have) a party.

Translate the following sentences into English.

1. 我不能许诺什么,但我将尽力而为。

2. 那不可能是玛丽,她在住院。

3. 此时他会在干什么呢?

4. 我可以用一下你的电话吗?

5. 他们可能正在车站等候。

6. 那支球队很可能赢得了足球赛,但我不知道,因为我没去。

7. 牛津近年来可能改变很多,但它仍是一座美丽的城市。

8. 如果情况是这样,我不妨一试。

9. 警察让所有的车都停下来,他们准是在搜寻逃犯。

10. 我今天一定要记住去银行。

PART III TOWARD PRODUCTIVE LANGUAGE

Read the following very quickly and try to get the general meaning; do not worry if you come across some new words.

青少年在青春期经历的身心变化有时会使自己与父母及成年人之间的沟通陷入困境,如何克服沟通上的障碍,请看本文提供的建议。

Text B

Talking to Your Parents

You got the lead in the school play and you can't wait to tell someone how excited you are. Who's the first person you go to at a moment like this? If you're like most boys and girls, you're more likely to share your feelings with a friend than your parents.

5 When you were younger, your mother and father were the first people you shared your good news with—and your problems. So what happened? Why is it that talking with your parents was so easy then and yet it's so hard now?

Changes That Affect Communication during Adolescence

It's not just your body that develops during puberty. Your mind is growing too. And this emotional development affects your relationships. Just as you've noticed how some friendships

10 deepen while others end, the longstanding relationships you have with people like parents are going to change too. It's all about establishing the unique identity and interests that will turn you into an independent adult.

People's minds develop in several ways during

15 their teenage years. Not only is this a time when you

lead /liːd / *n.* 主角,主要演员
be likely to 有可能
adolescence /ˌædəʊ'lesəns/ *n.* 青春期
puberty /'pjuːbəti/ *n.* 青春期
longstanding /'lɒŋ'stændɪŋ/ *adj.* 持久的
establish /ɪs'tæblɪʃ *vt.* 建立,成立
unique /juː'niːk/ *adj.* 独一无二的,仅有的,唯一的
identity /aɪ'dentɪti/ *n.* 身份;个性;特性
teenage /'tiːneɪdʒ/ *adj.* 青少年的

52

develop better problem-solving skills and the ability to make reasonable choices, you're also examining different values and beliefs and engaging in more self-discovery than at any other time in your life.

20 To achieve a sense of separation, some boys and girls may find themselves disagreeing with, clashing with, and rebelling against their parents for a time. Others may want to voice their opinions but keep them suppressed because they don't want to make a parent unhappy. All of these changes are confusing to someone who's used to having a close relationship with a parent or other adults. So how can you make sure your voice is heard?

Keep the Lines of Communication Open

25 The best tool you can use in communicating with parents—or any adult—is to keep talking to them, no matter what. Strong relationships depend heavily on keeping the lines of communication open (think of your close friends and how much you talk). Try to talk about everyday things with your parents as a way of building a connection. That doesn't mean telling them everything. In fact, turn the focus onto them for a change: ask about their day—just as they do with you.

30 Another way is to offer some information on your own. This puts the communication in your hands. The more you keep adults known about everyday things—even things like who drove you to the cinema—the less they need to ask. Communicating everyday things has another advantage: it can show your parents that you're grown-up and responsible enough to make good decisions.

35 It won't always be easy. You may get frustrated at times. But try not to give up. It may take a bit for a parent who is used to making all the decisions to adjust to the independent-thinking person their child is becoming. Parents are more likely to think of their children as grown up—and, as a result, capable of making more important decisions—when
40 they see them acting maturely. Parents also don't want to see their sons and daughters suffer if the choices they make on their own aren't the "right" ones. To many parents, it seems easier to step in and take

clash with 发生冲突;与……不协调
rebel against 反抗
suppress /sə'pres/ vt. 抑制(感情等),忍住;
压制;镇压
confusing /kən'fjuːzɪŋ/ adj. 令人困惑的
no matter 无论
in one's hands 由某人支配 / 控制 / 掌管
frustrated /'frʌstreɪtɪd/ adj. 挫败的,失望
的,泄气的
be / get used to 习惯于……的
step in 干涉,介入

control simply because they believe their years of
experience put them in a better position to make
decisions.

interaction /ˌɪntərˈækʃən/ *n.* 互动,相互作用
argumentative /ˌɑːɡjʊˈmentətɪv/ *adj.* 好辩的,争论的
chore /ˈtʃɔː/ *n.* 零工,杂务;令人疲劳不愉快的工作

How to Disagree with Your Parents

Using respectful language and behavior in your
everyday interactions is important. Don't shout at your parents and you'll have a much better
chance of getting what you want.

Of course, some parents are better than others at helping you to communicate well. Parents can
help by listening to and respecting your point of view, even if it opposes their own. If your parents
just don't seem to be on the same side as you, try these tips for disagreeing constructively:

● Don't make it personal. If you get unhappy, try to remember you're angry at the idea or
concept your parent or another adult is raising, not the person.

● Disagree without disrespect. Avoid laughing at your parents' ideas and beliefs. Instead of
saying "That's a stupid idea," try "I don't agree, and here's why."

● Use "I" sentences to communicate how you feel, what you think, and what you want or need.
Using "you" sentences can sound argumentative. For example, telling your mom or dad, "You
always remind me about my chores on Wednesdays when you know I have a lot of homework" has
a very different effect from "I'm feeling pressured because I have a lot of homework tonight. Can I
do those chores tomorrow?"

● Listen to the others' points of view. Doing so makes it more likely that a parent or adult will
listen to yours.

READING COMPREHENSION

A Choose the best answers for the following questions.

1. In paragraph 3, which change is not mentioned in affecting communication?

A. Your mind is growing.

B. You become taller and taller.

C. You develop better problem-solving skills and the ability to make reasonable choices.

D. Unique identity and interests turn you into an independent adult.

2. What does the underlined part in Paragraph 12 probably mean?

A. It is no easy task to express disagreement.

B. Respecting others means agreeing with others.

C. Expressing disagreement is disrespectful.

D. Show respect when expressing disagreement.

3. If you show your respect in your everyday actions, your parents will think _____.

A. they are too old to teach you

B. you are old enough to make your own decisions

C. their beliefs are being challenged

D. you are setting an example for them

4. Which of the following is a good example to express your disagreement according to the passage?

A. I am very tired now. Shall I do it later?

B. You make me nervous. Can you speak less?

C. I don't believe you at all.

D. You always forbid me to watch TV.

5. The passage is mainly about _____.

A. how to show respect for your parents

B. how to win the respect of your parents

C. how to express your disagreement with your parents

D. how to deal with your strict parents

B Answer the following questions.

1. Who did you share your good news with when you were very young?

2. What changes have taken place when you are turning into an independent adult?

3. What can we do to have a close relationship with our parents?

4. How to disagree with your parents according to the author?

5. How do you get along with your parents as an adult?

Unit 4

PART I PREPARATORY

WORDS AND PHRASES IN CONTEXT

Read aloud the following sentences, paying attention to the meaning of the words or phrases in italics.

1. Janet's been under a lot of *stress* since her mother's illness.

2. This job *makes a lot of demand on* my time.

3. Your encouragement will *stimulate* me to work more hard.

4. Her rash (鲁莽的) actions *manifested* a complete disregard for personal safety.

5. Illness *undermined* his strength.

6. My employer *countered* my request for more money by threatening to dismiss me.

7. We were *alert* to the dangers of the plan.

8. Noise outside *distracted* her mind from her studies.

9. The two countries have *maintained* friendly relations for many years.

10. The boss *exploded with* anger when he saw the sales report.

Write the meaning of each of the following words or phrases in the corresponding blank.   You can write either in English or in Chinese.

stress _____

make demand on _____

stimulate _____

manifest _____

undermine _____

counter _____

alert _____

distract _____

maintain _____

explode with _____

EXPRESSIONS IN CONTEXT

Study the following expressions and see how they are used in sentences.

regardless of 不管，不顾

◇ I shall go regardless of the weather.

cope with 对付……

◇ I cannot cope with that boy; he is stubborn.

concentrate on 专心于，把思想集中于

◇ Many firms are concentrating on increasing their markets overseas.

lead to 导致，引起；通向

◇ In given conditions, a bad thing can lead to good results.

play a part in 与……有关,对……有影响

◇ Cold winter played a part in my decision to stay in the north.

base on 使建立在……基础上

◇ We must base ourselves on the interests of the people.

bottle up 克制,遏制,抑制,约束

◇ They bottled up the submarines in their nest.

rather than (要)……而不……;与其……倒不如……

◇ We'll have the meeting in the classroom rather than in the auditorium.

EXPRESSIONS LEARNED IN DISPLAY

Complete each of the following sentences with the expressions you have just learned.

1. _____ being punished, he should be rewarded.

2. One should always _____ one's opinion _____ facts.

3. The question of cost will _____ important _____ our decision.

4. Traffic _____ in the tunnel.

5. All roads _____ Rome.

6. The factory _____ very well _____ the sudden increase in demand.

7. This year the company _____ improving its efficiency.

8. They decorated the house _____ the cost.

PART II   LANGUAGE IN CONTEXT

Read the following summary in Chinese and think what you are going to read in this text.

> 随着社会的进步,高科技突飞猛进的发展,人们的生活节奏日趋加快,社会竞争越来越激烈。优者生存,劣者淘汰使得人们面对不断变迁的事物时常出现不知所措的紧张心理和压力。这是社会文明的必然产物,但又是适应社会和环境不得不克服的心理状态。怎样才能克服紧张心理、应对压力呢?本文就向我们介绍了几种克服紧张心理和应对压力的方法。

PREVIEW QUESTIONS

Work in pairs or groups and discuss the following questions.

1. Are you often under stress in your life? Why or why not?

2. How is stress related to our health?

3. How do you handle stress in your life?

READING SELECTION

Text A

Ways of Handling Stress

The word *stress* is used to describe both external events that make demand on us and the internal responses they trigger. In fact, stress is the body's general response to any demand made on it, regardless of whether that demand is pleasant or unpleasant, or whether it is emotional or physical.

5   All of us need some amount of challenge in our daily life to keep ourselves stimulated and lead our lives to the fullest. Damaging stress occurs when challenges become impossible to cope with. The effect of excessive stress can manifest itself in a variety of ways; it can cause potentially harmful changes in the behavior and undermine both physical and mental health.   The following are some of the simple and effective ways of handling stress.

10   **Learning to relax:**   Relaxation helps reduce stress by distracting your mind from stress provoking thoughts.   Various relaxation techniques help to counter effects of "fight or flight" reaction. There are two main techniques

15 and both are easily learned. Practice them either lying down or sitting in a straight backed chair, with your feet flat and your hands relaxing on your laps. Spend 15 minutes on each—preferably after work or just before going to bed.

20   ***Progressive Muscular Relaxation (PMR)***—Close your eyes and direct your attention to each part of your body in turn.   As you do so, tense the muscle of the area and hold for 5

stress /stres/ *n.* 压力；紧张
external /ɪk'stɜːnl/ *adj.* 外面的，外部的
make demand on 提出要求，有求于
trigger /'trɪɡə/ *vt.* 引发，引起(连锁反应)
emotional /ɪ'məʊʃənəl/ *adj.* 感情上的；令人动情的
challenge /'tʃælɪndʒ/ *n.* 挑战
stimulate /'stɪmjʊleɪt/ *vt.* 刺激；激励
cope with（成功地）应付；妥善地处理
excessive /ɪk'sesɪv/ *adj.* 过度的；过分的；极度的
manifest /'mænɪfest/ *vt.* 清楚表示；显露
potentially /pə'tenʃəli/ *adv.* 潜在地；有可能地
undermine /ˌʌndə'maɪn/ *vt.* 暗中破坏；逐渐削弱
distract /dɪ'strækt/ *vt.* 使(人)分心；分散(注意力)
provoking /prə'vəʊkɪŋ/ *adj.* 激怒的，挑动的
counter /'kaʊntə/ *vt. & vi.* 对抗；反驳
reaction /rɪ'ækʃən/ *n.* 反应；回应
lap /læp/ *n.* (坐着时)膝上腰下的大腿部分
preferably /'prefərəbli/ *adv.* 更适宜地
progressive /prə'ɡresɪv/ *adj.* 逐步的；渐次的；循序渐进的
muscular /'mʌskjʊlə/ *adj.* (有关)肌(肉)的；强壮的

seconds, then release and totally relax the muscles. Concentrate on the sensation of warmth and
heaviness you will experience for about 10 seconds.

Deep Muscular Relaxation (DMR)—Use the same routine as for PMR, but without tensing. Focus only on relaxing by directing your attention to each set of muscles in turn, feeling them become weak and heavy.

Meditation: Meditation techniques allow us to achieve a deep state of calmness and serenity while remaining alert. It also causes the oxygen requirement, breathing rate, heart rate and blood pressure to drop and help muscles to relax. There are different techniques including so-called "Mindfulness" Meditation and Visualization. For example, imagine a pleasant, peaceful scene, such as sunny, deserted beach. Close your eyes and concentrate on all the colors, smells and sounds. Put yourself in the picture in a relaxed position. Continue imagining for 10—15 minutes. If practiced regularly, it can also lead to a more relaxed general view of life.

Exercise, balanced diet can play an enormous part in reducing stress, as well as help in maintaining body fitness. A number of times aches and pains complained in the neck, shoulder and back are a result of poor posture and mental tension. Performing some stretching exercises or regular exercise pattern can help you combat stress. Similarly a healthy balanced diet based on cereals, fruits and vegetables can help provide body with all the essential nutrients necessary for survival. Deficiency of various vitamins and mineral can exhibit a number of symptoms which might lead to mental and physical stress.

Letting off steam is another good way of relieving stress or tension. It is best to express

release /rɪ'liːs/ **vt.** 释放；放开
sensation /sen'seɪʃən/ **n.** 感觉；感受
meditation /ˌmedɪ'teɪʃən/ **n.** 默想；沉思
serenity /sɪ'renəti/ **n.** 安详；宁静
alert /ə'lɜːt/ **adj.** 警惕的，警觉的，注意的
oxygen requirement 需氧量
visualization /ˌvɪzjʊəlaɪ'zeɪʃən/ **n.** 形象化，想象
deserted /dɪ'zɜːtɪd/ **adj.** 荒芜的，人迹罕至的
balanced diet **n.** 均衡的饮食
enormous /ɪ'nɔːməs/ **adj.** 巨大的，极大的
maintain /meɪn'teɪn/ **vt.** 保持；继续
posture /'pɒstʃə/ **n.** 姿势；态度
tension /'tenʃən/ **n.** 紧张；张力；拉力
cereal /'sɪərɪəl/ **n.** 谷类植物；谷物
nutrient /'njuːtrɪənt/ **n.** (食品或化学品)营养物，营养品
deficiency /dɪ'fɪʃənsi/ **n.** 缺乏，不足
vitamin /'vaɪtəmɪn/ **n.** 维生素
mineral /'mɪnərəl/ **n.** 矿物质；矿石
symptom /'sɪmptəm/ **n.** 症状；征兆

your frustration or anger when it occurs. If you always bottle things up, you are more likely to suffer from physical illness associated with stress or to explode with
55 pent-up rage. If you want to yell to let off steam, go somewhere such as a basement or a garden, where you cannot easily disturb others.

Change of routine: Breaking routine helps to remove the stress that is bound into your personal rituals. Pick up
60 a small gift for yourself or a loved one on the way. And when you arrive, don't always do the same thing. If you usually sit down in front of the TV with a drink, try doing 10 minutes' exercise and taking a shower first. Similarly, on weekends it is just as important to vary your activities
65 as much as you can.

Change your response: One of the best, but most difficult, stress relieving strategy is to change your response to the events around you. You are the only person who can improve your attitude and performance. There is no sense in blaming other people or past events for everything that goes wrong. You might get sympathy, but you
70 will not achieve the results you want.

Once your stress-inducing problems have been clearly identified, you can think out a wide range of possible solutions, rejecting those that you know from experience do not work. Focus on the quality of the effort involved rather than the amount of the solution.

frustration /frʌˈstreɪʃ ə n/ *n.* 挫败，挫折，受挫
bottle up 克制，抑制，约束
explode with 突然发作
pent-up /ˈpentˈʌp/ *adj.* 被压抑的，被抑制的
yell /jel/ *vt. & vi.* 叫喊
let off steam 宣泄被压抑的感情；发牢骚；散发多余的精力
basement /ˈbeɪsmənt/ *n.* 地下室
routine /ruːˈtiːn/ *n.* 例行公事，惯例，惯常的程序
ritual /ˈrɪtʃʊəl/ *n.* (宗教等的)仪式；例行公事
shower /ˈʃaʊə/ *n.* 淋浴
strategy /ˈstrætɪdʒi/ *n.* 战略；策略
sympathy /ˈsɪmpəθi/ *n.* 同情(心)
inducing /ɪnˈdjuːsɪŋ/ *adj.* 产生诱导作用的
identify /aɪˈdentɪfaɪ/ *vt.* 识别；确定
reject /rɪˈdʒekt/ *vt.* 拒绝；摈弃
focus on 集中注意力于；使聚焦于

COMPREHENSION CHECK

Understanding the General Ideas

Discuss the following questions in pairs or groups. The key words given in the brackets may help you in your discussion.

1. What is stress?

   (response, demand, regardless of, pleasant, unpleasant, emotional, physical)

2. Why does the author present to us some simple and effective ways of handling stress?

   (damaging, harmful, behavior, undermine, physical, mental)

3. How can we get relaxed according to the author?

   (close, direct, tense, release, concentrate on, routine)

4. What are the ways the author presents to handle stress?

   (relax, meditate, exercise, balanced diet, routine, response)

5. What is the type of text of this passage?

   (narrative, descriptive, expositive, argumentative)

Understanding the Specifics

Read the following sentences and tell if they are true or false according to the text. In the brackets leading each statement, put "T" for true or "F" for false.

1. (   ) Any external demand made on the body will trigger general internal responses.
2. (   ) It is certain that any challenge in our daily life results in physical and psychological diseases.
3. (   ) DMR is different from PMR in that it is unnecessary to tense the muscle in the latter.
4. (   ) The author cites the example in the 6th paragraph to show how to use meditation techniques.

5. (   ) Mental and physical stress may result from lack of various vitamins and minerals.

6. (   ) If you never let off steam, you are sure to suffer from physical illness.

7. (   ) We'd better try our best to do different things on weekends to remove the stress.

8. (   ) The author tends to agree that it is no use crying over spilt milk.

STUDY AND PRACTICE

Vocabulary

Fill in the blanks with the words below. Change the form where necessary.

progressive	sensation	maintain	identify	strategy
external	alert	symptom	reject	stimulate

1. The _____ features of the building are very attractive.

2. The book _____ her imagination.

3. Seeing him again after so many years was a strange _____ .

4. He is a man _____ to the problems.

5. He has to _____ his wife and two children.

6. The doctor told her to watch out for _____ of measles.

7. I admired the general who was a master of _____ .

8. Would you be able to _____ the man who robbed you?

9. He was afraid she would _____ him because he was a foreigner.

10. This is a _____ course in English study.

Expressions

Rewrite the following sentences with the help of the phrases and expressions provided. The italicized part in each sentence may serve as the hint for your task. The first sentence is done for you.

rather than	cope with	regardless of	make demand on
bottle up	lead to	play a part in	base... on

1. The work *takes up a lot of* my time.

   This work makes a lot of demand on my time.

2. Our development plans *are grounded on* the results of our market research.

   _____

3. You should be working *instead of* lying there in bed.

   _____

4. There was no understanding person to talk to, so Fred got his unhappy feelings *pent up*.

   _____

5. The unsatisfactory conditions *resulted in* a sit-down strike.

   _____

6. The teacher *plays a very active role in* this type of classroom activities.

   _____

7. She was unable *to deal successfully with* the duties of her new position.

   _____

8. Some people act impulsively, *taking no account of* what will happen afterwards.

Translation

A From Chinese to English

1. 她的行动表明她全然不顾个人安危。

2. 把狗放开, 它已被拴了好几个钟头了。

3. 有什么烦恼事告诉我们, 别憋在心里!

4. 这些事件会严重影响对警方的支持。

5. 她把兔子从陷阱中放了出去。

6. 这种制度的缺陷不久就变得很明显。

7. 这部电影激发了公众对这次灾难中受难者的同情。

8. 他担心她会因他不是本国人而拒绝他。

B From English to Chinese

1. In fact, stress is the body's general response to any demand made on it, regardless of whether that demand is pleasant or unpleasant, or whether it is emotional or physical.

2. Damaging stress occurs when challenges become impossible to cope with. The effect of excessive stress can manifest itself in a variety of ways;   it can cause potentially harmful changes in the behavior and undermine both physical and mental health.

3. Meditation techniques allow us to achieve a deep state of calmness and serenity while remaining alert.

4. A number of times aches and pains complained in the neck, shoulder and back are a result of poor posture and mental tension.

5. Once your stress-inducing problems have been clearly identified, you can think out a wide range of possible solutions, rejecting those that you know from experience do not work.

Modal Auxiliaries (情态动词) (Ⅱ)

4）ought to 的意义和用法

(1) 表示应该

You ought to buy a new pair of shoes.

You ought to leave early tomorrow morning.

ought to +不定式完成体表示过去应做某事而实际未做,如:

You ought to have helped him (but you did not).

He ought to have been more careful. (He was not careful enough.)

(2) 表示推测,与 must 基本同义,只是意义比 must 有所弱化,试比较:

Mary Blake must be home by now.

Mary Blake ought to be home by now.

前句用 must 含义是根据她动身的时间、路程远近、列车速度等具体条件,断定她现在已经到家了。后句用 ought to 含义是想她该到家了,但是否已到不能肯定。

5）will 的意义和用法

(1) 表示意愿

My sister will help you.

I will (I'll) lend you the book if you need it. (=I'm willing to...)

will 用于第二、三人称疑问句是询问别人是否愿意做某事,如:

Will you have some tea?

Will you sing at the concert tomorrow evening?

(2) 表示意图

I will write to her tomorrow.

Why will you go there?

6) need 的意义和用法

need 表示"需要"或"必须"限用于否定句和疑问句,如:

You needn't do it again.

Need he do his homework first?

在否定句中,可以用 need 的否定形式+不定式完成体表示已经做了不必要做的事,如:

We needn't have hurried.

You needn't have said that when he asked.

needn't 后的不定式也能用进行体或被动语态,如:

We needn't be standing in the rain. We can take shelter in the hut over there.

The hedges needn't be trimmed this week.

7) dare 的意义和用法

dare 表示"胆敢",通常用于否定陈述句或疑问句,如:

I dare not go there.

I don't know whether he dare try.

How dare he say such rude things about me?

8) used to 的意义和用法

在陈述句中,used to 表示过去事态或过去习惯,如:

Edward Coke used to be an army officer.

He used to walk miles after breakfast.

在疑问句、否定陈述句或强调句中,可以有两种形式,如:

Used you to go to the same school as Edward?

Did you use to go to the same school as Edward?

I usedn't to smoke.

I didn't use to smoke.

在附加疑问或简略回答中,也可以有两种形式,如:

John used to be very fat, didn't he?/use(d)n't he?

A: Used you to go to school in Australia?

B: Yes, I did. / Yes, I used to.

used to 表示过去习惯动作或过去经常发生的事态,通常可以不带时间状语,但有时根据语义意图也可与频度状语或某些表示过去时间的状语搭配,如:

He used to go and see his children on Sundays.

He used to play football before his marriage.

如果时间状语是表示一个特定的时间或时段,则往往不能与 used to 搭配,不可以说:

* He used to live in London for five years.

* He used to go and see her last Sunday.

IMMEDIATE PRACTICE

Fill in the blanks with the modal auxiliaries you've just learned.

1. You _____ (read) this book. It's marvelous!

2. We _____ (pack) our thick clothes. The weather was really warm.

3. They were so frightened that they _____ (go) into the room.

4. Let's look at it again, _____ ?

5. By this time next year she _____ (take) her university degree.

6. Bring me the papers, _____ ?

7. I _____ (live) in Nanjing, but now I live in Shanghai.

8. _____ I carry your suitcase?

9. A lion _____ (attack) a man only when hungry.

10. _____ you help me lift this box?

Translate the following sentences into English.

1. 你应当更多地探望你的父母。

2. 在红绿灯前他们本应停车。

3. 如果你太忙就不必来开会了。

4. 她不敢说出她的想法。

5. 明天我将给你个明确的回答。

6. 我们到哪里去度假？

7. 妈妈过去常常在暑假的时候去乡下。

8. 把油倒在水上，油会漂在上面。

9. 你可以不用来这么早，晚会八点钟才开始。

10. 经理的脾气如此暴躁以至没人敢告诉他这个坏消息。

PART III TOWARD PRODUCTIVE LANGUAGE

Read the following very quickly and try to get the general meaning; do not worry if you come across some new words.

> 社会的迅速发展使得人们的生活节奏加快,人们在学习、工作、婚恋和家庭生活等方面普遍感到了沉重的压力,出现了心理、生理失调,影响身心健康;或由于不了解心理紧张如何调控,出现了社会适应不良,生命质量下降。因此,了解心理紧张产生的原因及其症状并进行相应的自我调控是非常必要的。

Text B

Stress

The way in which damaging stress manifests itself in the body varies from one individual to another. One of the important aspect of dealing with stress is knowing the way in which your body responds to the challenges that are too severe. These reactions are automatic and subconscious and might range from being irritable to overeating, breaking out in lives, developing a migraine headache
5 or having heartburn. However, once you understand stresses operating in your life, you can begin to cope with them. Slowly you will realize with practice that it is possible to control stress-related symptoms in a varied number of weeks.

10 When our body is subjected to stress over a long period of time, it remains in a prolonged state of preparedness for flight or fight. Blood pressure is permanently raised, continuing muscle tension leads

severe /sɪ'vɪə/ *adj.* 严重的, 剧烈的
automatic /ɔːtə'mætɪk/ *adj.* 自动的;不假思索的;无意识的
subconscious /sʌb'kɒnʃəs/ *adj.* 下意识的,潜意识的
irritable /'ɪrɪtəbəl/ *adj.* 易怒的,急躁的
migraine /'miːɡreɪn/ *n.* 偏头痛
heartburn /'hɑːtbɜːn/ *n.* 胃灼热,烧心
subject to 使服从,使遭受
prolonged /prə'lɒŋd/ *adj.* 持续很久的,长时间的
permanently /'pɜːmənəntlɪ/ *adv.* 永久地;不变地

to digestive problem, pains and aches, and the body's resistance to disease remains suppressed.

15 **Causes of Stress**

Stress is nothing new, but the 20th century has produced many changes that have increased the amount of stress people experience.

Any change that upsets your accustomed pattern of life can cause stress.

Advances in technology have increased the pressure on everyone. In the age of speed and
20 instantaneous worldwide communication, there is greater need of quick responses than in the past. More decisions have to be made nowadays. The average person has a high degree of responsibility and accountability.

You have a wider range of choices at all levels of life, in work and in leisure.

Overcrowding, noise and pollution have resulted from an increase in population.

25 People have come to demand a higher quality of communication and understanding in all their relationships.

Technology has affected work, leisure, and social relationships. Human contacts are decreasing as a result.

Physicai Syptoms of Stress

30 Do you recognize two or more of the following in yourself or in someone close to you? If so, the problem needs to be tackled immediately.

Have your eating habits changed?

Has your sleep pattern altered?

Is your digestive system upset?

35 Have you developed any nervous habits, such as fidgeting or touching your hair and face repeatedly?

Is your blood pressure raised?

Do you have frequent headaches, cramps, and muscle spasms?

40 Have you become hyperactive?

Have your sexual performance, drive, and

accustomed /əˈkʌstəmd/ *adj.* 惯常的,习惯于……的
instantaneous /ˌɪnstənˈteɪnɪəs/ *adj.* 瞬间发生的, 即刻的
accountability /əˌkaʊntəˈbɪlɪtɪ/ *n.* 有责任,有义务;可说明性
muscle spasm 肌肉痉挛
hyperactive /haɪpəˈræktɪv/ *adj.* 活动过度的,极度活跃的,活动亢进的

enjoyment deteriorated?

Are you drinking or smoking more?

Has your child <u>reverted to</u> an earlier, outgrown habit, such as bedwetting, temper tantrums, or

45 thumb sucking?

Mental Symptoms of Stress

Do you recognize two or more of the following in yourself or in someone close to you? If so, stress might be reaching a potentially dangerous level. Remember, however, that these can also be symptoms of other problems, such as physical illness.

50 Have you begun to suffer from a phobia or obsession?

Have you lost self-confidence and self-esteem?

Do you constantly feel guilty?

Do you dread the future?

Have your memory and concentration deteriorated?

55 Do you find yourself unable to finish one task properly before having to rush on to the next?

Do you feel constantly irritable and angry?

Do you fill the day with trivial tasks?

Do you find it hard to make decisions?

Do you often cry or feel like crying?

60 Does your mind race so that you cannot focus on one task or thought?

The Natural Reaction to Stress

When confronted by acute physical or psychological stress, the brain triggers a chain reaction that prepares the body to fight the perceived threat or to flee from it. Though essential to survival in

65 life-threatening situations and often useful when dealing with challenges such as deadlines at work, the fight-or-flight response is less appropriate for dealing with more routine stresses. If triggered often enough, it can lead to serious health problems. These

70 are some of the effects:

deteriorate /dɪ'tɪərɪəreɪt/ *vi.* 恶化, 变坏
bedwetting *n.* 尿床, 遗尿
tantrum /'tæntrəm/ *n.* 突然发怒
phobia /'fəʊbɪə/ *n.* 恐惧, 厌恶
obsession /əb'seʃən/ *n.* 困扰; 无法摆脱的思想(或情感)
esteem /ɪ'stiːm/ *n.* 尊敬; 好评
trivial /'trɪvɪəl/ *adj.* 琐碎的, 没有价值的, 没有意义的
deadline /'dedlaɪn/ *n.* 最后期限

The brain perceives some form of impending danger.

Signals from the brain cause the adrenal glands to produce fight-or-flight hormones such as
75 adrenaline and noradrenaline, which speed up heart and breathing rates and muscle response.

Kidney function is reduced as less blood is available to the kidneys.

Muscle fibers contract to prepare for sudden
80 movement.

The pupils of the eyes dilate.

The salivary glands stop secreting saliva and the mouth feels dry.

Skin becomes pale as surface blood vessels contract to direct more blood to muscles.

Sweat production increases in order to counteract overheating.

85 Heart rate increases to supply more blood to muscles.

Blood pressure rises.

Breathing rate increases to supply more oxygen to muscles.

The liver increases its output of sugar and fat to fuel the muscles.

Digestion slows or ceases.

90 Tightened muscles stop urination and defecation.

impending /ɪm'pendɪŋ/ *adj.* 即将发生的，迫在眉睫的

adrenal /ə'driːnəl/ *adj.* 肾上的；肾上腺的

noradrenaline /ˌnɔːrə'drenəlɪn/ *n.* 去甲肾上腺素

dilate /daɪ'leɪt/ *vt. & vi.* (使某物)扩大，膨胀，张大

salivary gland *n.* 唾液腺

secrete /sɪ'kriːt/ *vt.* (尤指动物或植物器官)分泌；隐匿，隐藏

blood vessel 血管

counteract /kaʊntər'ækt/ *vt.* 对抗；抵消

urination /ˌjʊərɪ'neɪʃn/ *n.* 排尿

defecation /defə'keɪʃn/ *n.* 澄清，净化；通便

READING COMPRENENSION

A Choose the best answers for the following questions.

1. According to the text, one can cope with stresses _____.

　A. once stresses operate in his or her life

　B. once one understands stresses operating in his or her life

C. once one's blood pressure is permanently raised

D. once one is subjected to stress over a long period of time

2. According to the text, all the following may be the causes of stress EXCEPT_____.

    A. advances in technology   B. decreasing human contact

    C. any upset in life   D. usual pattern of life

3. The underlined phrase "revert to" in line 44 most probably means _____.

    A. develop   B. go back to   C. form   D. break

4. All the following statements are true according to the passage EXCEPT_____.

    A. With practice stress-related symptoms can be controlled in a period of time.

    B. Mental stresses are likely to lead to physical illness.

    C. Under acute physical or psychological stress, we want to fight with someone.

    D. Stress might be reaching a potentially dangerous level if you have lost self-confidence, feel

        like crying, and dread the future.

5. In terms of controlling purposes, the text is _____.

    A. expositive   B. narrative   C. descriptive   D. argumentative

B **Answer the following questions.**

1. What are the causes of stress?

2. What are the physical symptoms of stress?

3. What are the mental symptoms of stress?

4. What are the natural reactions to stress?

5. Do you recognize in yourself two or more of the physical and mental symptoms of stress

   mentioned in the text? If so, how do you deal with them?

PART I   PREPARATORY

WORDS IN CONTEXT

Read aloud the following sentences, paying attention to the meaning of the words in italics.

1. We will *remain* in regular contact with them.

2. Bob is over the hill as a *professional* athlete.

3. Who *spread* these rumors?

4. A little neglect may *breed* great mischief.

5. The progress of the society is based on *harmony*.

6. The stronger man *dominates* the weaker.

7. The sun *emerged* from behind the cloud.

8. In history, change is *constant*.

9. He was busy *assembling* the bike.

10. This machine is the *ancestor* of the modern computer.

Write the meaning of each of the following words in the corresponding blank. You can write either in English or in Chinese.

remain _____

professional _____

spread _____

breed _____

harmony _____

dominate _____

emerge _____

constant _____

assemble _____

ancestor _____

EXPRESSIONS IN CONTEXT

Study the following expressions and see how they are used in sentences.

date back to 追溯于

◇ The history of hockey can date back to thousands of years ago.

come into being 存在；形成

◇ When did the club first come into being?

break up 关系破裂；解散；结束

◇ We don't know the reason why they have broken up with each other.

in the wake of 尾随，紧跟，仿效

◇ There were a lot of fallen trees in the wake of the storm.

to...degree 达到……程度

◇ Criticism is not lost on you to some degree.

owe to 应该感谢；把……归功于

◇ Owing to his hard work, he succeeded.

rely on 信赖，依赖

◇ We must believe in and rely on the masses.

go through 经历；浏览；检查；完成

◇ Their success went through lots of difficulties.

EXPRESSIONS LEARNED IN DISPLAY

Complete each of the following sentences with the expressions you have just learned.

1. When did the Roman Empire _____ ?

2. Traders came _____ the conquering armies.

3. The party _____ and the neighbors hurried home.

4. You can _____ me for help.

5. The basic ideas of this theory _____ the 1960s.

6. _____ , I do agree with Mr. Smith.

7. We _____ a great deal _____ our parents.

8. China _____ great changes in the past 60 years.

PART II LANGUAGE IN CONTEXT

GET YOURSELF INTERESTED

Read the following summary in Chinese and think what you are going to read in this text.

随着流行音乐越来越精致,民间的唱歌热也逐渐演变成一种文化消费习惯后,一大批新生代的年轻人几乎是握着麦克风长大的,"K 歌"是他们生活中重要的一环,他们取代了当年只听不唱的老一辈,凭借从小熏染的对流行的敏感和认知,成为流行音乐听众的中坚力量。然而你对流行音乐的发展了解多少呢?

PREVIEW QUESTIONS

Work in pairs or groups and discuss the following questions.

1. Do you like pop music?

2. What kind of pop music do you like?

3. Who is your favorite singer? Why do you like him or her?

4. What kind of effect does music have on you?

5. Do you agree that music is a universal language?

READING SELECTION

Text A

A Brief History of Pop Music

Pop is short for popular, and it's remained the defining term for the ever-changing music favoured by the public. Although not specifically applied until the middle of the 20th century, pop music can be traced back to a few decades before that.

The Early Days

5 　You could say that the songs of music hall were the first real pop songs, written by professionals and widely performed for audiences. That dates back to the Victorian era, when a performer needed a catchy, identifiable song. Things changed with the coming of recording, early in the 20th century. With that, music had the chance to be much more widely spread, because records were relatively cheap. In America, that led to a breed of professional songwriters in New

10 York who wrote pieces intended to be recorded and sell well—Tin Pan Alley. London had its own songwriters as the music business became centered on Denmark Street in the West End.

The Crooners

The first major pop stars as such were the crooners of the 1930s and '40s. Bing Crosby sold millions of records, as did Frank Sinatra

15 (arguably the first modern pop star, with lots of screaming teenage female fans). They recorded and performed with full orchestras in the main style of the day. But there were other vocals groups, such as the Mills Brothers and the

20 Inkspots, whose harmonies set the standards for those seeking fame. As the style known as swing became popular, big bands also came into

remain /rɪˈmeɪn/ **n.** 剩余物；残余 **vi.** 保持；逗留

trace back to 追溯到……

professional /prəˈfeʃənəl/ **adj.** 职业的，专业的 **n.** 具有某专业资格的人，专业人士

date back to 回溯至

era /ˈɪərə/ **n.** 纪元；历史时期，时代

identifiable /aɪˈdentɪfaɪəbəl/ **adj.** 可以确认的，可以识别的

breed /briːd/ **n.** 种，种类，品种

crooner /ˈkruːnə/ **n.** 低声唱歌的人或歌手

orchestra /ˈɔːkɪstrə/ **n.** 管弦乐队

harmony /ˈhɑːmənɪ/ **n.** 和谐，协调

their own, with tunes like Glen Miller's "In the Mood" becoming standards.

The Charts

Curiously, pop music charts didn't exist until 1952, when the first Top Twenty was recorded. It came at an interesting time, as "teenagers" really came into being. Historically there'd been no transitional period between childhood and adulthood. Now, after World War II, that seemed to begin, imported from America, teens found their music. Rock'n'roll brought much more of that, and Elvis Presley became a global star, the biggest of the late 1950s and early 1960s. But he would find himself replaced by the Beatles, who revolutionized pop by writing their own material, causing a fashion that remained forever. The Beatles set the standard for pop music, and beatlesque has become a standard descriptive adjective. From 1962 until their break up in 1970 they dominated the charts in Britain and America.

Post Beatles

The Beatles influenced a generation—more than one, really—with their melodies and harmonies, and that was apparent in the 1970s, when pop went through several styles, from the Glam Rock to Punk. But the biggest pop star to emerge from the period was a singer and pianist, Elton John, whose popularity has remained constant.

The idea of artists writing their own material remained in the wake of the Fab Four, although professional songwriters stayed in demand for those unable to pen a tune. From the early days of rock there had been "manufactured" stars—people taken on board for a pretty face rather than any talent, and made into stars by producers. It had happened to Adam Faith, Alvin Stardust and many others, most of whom only enjoyed short careers. The 1980s proved a still decade for pop. Styles came and went, but it was an era short on memorable music. Only Wham (and later George Michael) emerged as true pop stars.

Boy Bands

The 1990s was the time of boy bands. A group of young male singers was assembled for their looks, given catchy songs and arrangements and pushed to

transitional /træn'zɪʃənəl/ *adj.* 变迁的;过渡期的

break up 结束;破裂

dominate /'dɒmɪneɪt/ *vt. & vi.* 控制,统治;耸立于,俯临

constant /'kɒnstənt/ *adj.* 恒久不变的;不断的

in the wake of 尾随,紧跟,仿效

the Fab Four 指披头士乐队

manufacture /ˌmænjə'fæktʃə/ *vt.* 制造;捏造

assemble /ə'sembəl/ *vt.& vi.* 集合,收集 *vt.* 装配,组合

fame. It happened to East 17 and, the most memorably Take That. America saw how it worked and gave the world the Backstreet Boys and 'N Sync, and for a few years it worked very well, selling millions of records.

55 But like any fashion, it passed. A female version, the Spice Girls, was briefly huge. Obviously, the only ones to come out of this and sustain a solo career was Robbie Williams from Take That and Justin Timberlake from 'N Sync. America tried a similar tactic with female pop stars, and both Mariah Carey and Britney Spears became massive manufactured stars, followed, to a lesser degree, by

60 Christina Aguilera.

The New Millennium

Since the year 2000 there's been fewer major new stars, relying mostly on established talent. Several younger artists have come and gone, and new styles have briefly emerged, but nothing appears to have gained a major position besides modern R&B, which owes little to its

65 soulful ancestors, but a lot to hip-hop—which itself has become a pop style.

---

sustain /sə'steɪn/ *vt.* 长期保持；使继续
tactic /'tæktɪk/ *n.* 方法，策略
owe sth to sb 欠……(某物)；应该感谢；把 ……归功于
ancestor /'ænsəstə/ *n.* 祖先；原型；先驱

COMPREHENSION CHECK

Understanding the General Ideas

Discuss the following questions in pairs or groups. The key words given in the brackets may help you in your discussion.

1. What does pop stand for?

    (popular, ever-changing music, favored, the public)

2. What was the first real pop song?

    (written by professionals, widely performed for audiences, Victorian era)

3. Why did the music have the chance to be much more widely spread?

   (coming of recording, relatively cheap)

4. Who were the first major pop stars ?

   (crooners of the 1930s and '40s)

5. When did pop music charts exist?

   (until 1952)

Understanding the Specifics

Read the following sentences and tell if they are true or false according to the text. In the brackets leading each statement, put "T" for true or "F" for false.

1. (   ) Pop music can be traced back to a few decades ago.

2. (   ) Historically there'd been no transitional period between childhood and adulthood for the pop music charts.

3. (   ) Beatles was replaced by Elvis Presley in the late 50s and early 60s.

4. (   ) Beatles broke up in 1962.

5. (   ) From the early days of rock there had been "manufactured" stars.

6. (   ) In 1990s, the boy bands were a group of young male singers assembled for their beautiful voice.

7. (   ) Since the year 2000 there's been fewer major new stars, relying mostly on established talent.

8. (   ) Hip-hop itself is not a pop style.

STUDY AND PRACTICE

Vocabulary

Fill in the blanks with the words below. Change the form where necessary.

remain	breed	harmony	dominate
emerge	constant	manufacture	assemble
ancestor	sustain		

1. You have to _____ objective about these things.

2. Rabbits _____ quickly.

3. The couple lives in perfect _____.

4. The skyscraper _____ the city.

5. The sun _____ from behind the cloud.

6. In our world nothing seems _____.

7. She _____ a false story to hide the facts.

8. Over 10,000 people were _____ at the airport to honor the President's visit.

9. The facts _____ his theory.

10. She has worshipped her _____.

Expressions

Rewrite the following sentences with the help of the phrases and expressions provided. The italicized part in each sentence may serve as the hint for your task. The first sentence is done for you.

in the wake of	break up	to...degree	owe to
rely on	go through	come into being	date back

1. He is *indebted* more *to* luck than to ability *for* his success..

He owe his success more to luck than to ability.

2. The castle can *be traced back to* the 14th century.

3. New companies *come into existence* every year.

4. Outbreak of disease occurred *following* the drought.

5. We can always *depend on* our parents when we are in trouble.

6. The ice began to *fall apart* on the river.

7. She's *experienced* a difficult time recently.

8. I agree with you *to some extent*.

Translation

A From Chinese to English

1. 滴水穿石。

2. 凡是用这种策略的都获得了成功。

3. 这个生产塑料袋的工厂要倒闭了。

4. 崇拜祖先的风俗在这些人中是普遍的。

5. 我很感激我的妻子和孩子。

6. 流行音乐的兴起可以追溯到上个世纪的早期。

7. 披头士的音乐影响了一代人甚至是几代人。

8. 一些年轻的艺术家在舞台上只是昙花一现。

B From English to Chinese

1. As the style known as swing became popular, big bands also came into their own.

2. The Beatles set the standard for pop music, and beatlesque has become a standard descriptive adjective.

3. But the biggest pop star to emerge from the period was a singer and pianist, Elton John.

4. A group of young male singers was assembled for their looks, given catchy songs and arrangements and pushed to fame.

5. Since the year 2000 there's been fewer major new stars, relying mostly on established talent.

GRAMMAR

Modal Auxiliaries (情态动词) (III)

3. 情态动词使用中的几个问题

1) 情态动词过去时形式的意义与用法

与其他类型的动词不同,情态动词过去时形式不限于表示过去时间,有时表示现在时间,有时也可表示将来时间或过去将来时间,如:

I'm not sure; you might be right.

I'd like a cup of coffee.

Would you go with me tomorrow?

I asked him whether he would help me.

2）情态动词在间接引语中的用法

must, ought to, need, dare 没有过去时形式, 它们在间接引语中仍用原来形式。

如：

"You mustn't smoke in here."

→ I told him that he mustn't smoke in here.

"You ought to start at once."

→ He told me that I ought to start at once.

used to 只有过去时形式, 没有现在时形式, 在间接引语中不变。如：

"There used to be an old temple here."

→ He told us that there used to be an old temple here.

3）情态动词在非间接引语中的用法

在非间接引语中, 情态动词过去时形式的意义和用法情况比较复杂。一般说来, could 和 would 在直接引语中能用作相应于 can 和 will 的各种情态意义, 而 might 和 should 一般不能表示相应于 may 和 shall 的各种情态意义。

might 在非间接引语中一般不用于表示过去的可能, 更不用于表示过去的意愿或意图等。may not 表示"不许可"时, might not 并不表示过去的不许可, 试比较：

He may not go. (他不可以去。)

He might not go. (他也许不会去。)

表示过去的"不许可"通常是：

He was not allowed to go.

I didn't permit him to go.

表示过去的"可能", may 也并不等于 might, 试比较：

It may rain this evening. (今晚可能下雨, 表示将来的可能性。)

It might rain this evening. (今晚也许会下雨, 虽然也表示将来的可能性, 但可能性小些。)

如果要表示过去的可能性,可以用 may/might +不定式完成体,如:

He may/might have been hurt.

在这里用 may 或 might 基本上意义差不多,但用 might 语气比 may 婉转。

should 在非间接引语中所表示的情态意义与 shall 有时有所不同,试比较:

You shall stay with us as long as you like. (表示说话人的意愿)

You should stay with us as long as you like. (表示应该)

4)关于情态动词的推测性用法

大多数情态动词都有非推测性和推测性两种用法,主要区别在于:指客观情况的是非推测性用法,指说话人主观看法的是推测性用法,如:

We must be careful.

Smith must be very careless.

前一句(我们必须小心)中的情态动词指客观情况,是非推测性用法;后一句(史密斯想必十分粗心)中的情态动词指说话人的主观看法,是推测性看法。做推测性用法的情态动词一般都有以下这些句法特征:

(1) 其后的不定式可以采取完成体形式

You must have thought about that.

You must have been disappointed.

(2) 其后的不定式可以采取进行体形式

He must be working late at the office.

He must be calling tonight.

(3) 可用于 there- 存在句

There must be some mistake.

There must have been some mistake.

一般说来,做推测性用法的情态动词有 might, may, could, can, should, ought to, would, will, must 等。假如出现如下情景:

A 问 "There's someone at the door. Didn't you hear the bell?"

B 的回答可能是:

It might be George.

It may be George.

It could be George.

It should be George.

It ought to be George.

It would be George.

It will be George.

It must be George.

B 回答时仅是做揣测，表示各种可能性。一般来说，might 表示可能性程度最低，must 表示肯定程度最高，上列各句由低而高，依次类推。

IMMEDIATE PRACTICE

Fill in the blanks with the modal auxiliaries you've just learned.

1. Research findings show we spend about two hours dreaming every night, no matter what we _____ (do) during the day.

2. You _____ (see) her in her office last Friday; she's been out of town for two weeks.

3. —Well done, Tom!

    —Thanks, but given me more time, I _____ (do) it much better.

4. I promised to get there before 5 o'clock, but now the rain is pouring down. They _____ (wait) for me impatiently.

5. You _____ (go) to town to see the film yesterday. It will be on TV tonight.

6. _____ I _____ (be) free tomorrow, I will come.

7. When my parents were away, my grandmother _____ (look after) me.

8. We _____ (study) last night, but we went to the concert instead.

9. She _____ (be) home last night, because I saw her car parked at the gate of her house.

10. We _____ (receive) the letter yesterday, but it didn't arrive.

Translate from Chinese into English.

1. 如果我们是男人，我们现在会采取一些行动。

2. 我们本应先核对一下时间再动身的。

3. 如果我真有心这样做，我是可以挣些钱的。

4. 她告诉我她今年冬天可能去夏威夷。

5. 你当时准是在想什么心事。

6. 现在水应该开了。

7. 她其实不必亲自来的，写封信就够了。

8. 她讲的不可能是真话。

9. 万一还疼，就再吃一片这个药。

10. 那时她不可能超过六岁。

PART III TOWARD PRODUCTIVE LANGUAGE

Read the following very quickly and try to get the general meaning; do not worry if you come acorss some new words.

近年来有许多科学家通过科学研究证实,音乐对人的身心健康有着积极的作用,音乐还有很多奇妙的功能。音乐治疗法已经在很多国家盛行,医学界通过临床实验认定,音乐对放松身心、振作精神、诱发睡眠等,都很有实效。为什么音乐会有如此神奇的效果呢？音乐疗法是不是适用于所有的人呢？本文将给你一些解答。

Text B

Music and Health

Think of the last time a song really moved you, or meant something to you. Listening to and playing music stimulates many different sections of the brain, affecting us physically as well. Have you ever thought why we as humans are so connected to music?

Music has unending benefits on our health. It has been proven that music reduces blood
5 pressure. Scientists are currently testing the effects of playing music games with dyslexics, and how it may improve their reading ability. Music is used to calm Alzheimer's patients and others with age-related diseases in hospitals and nursing homes, helping to reduce and control conflicts.

Music is commonly used as a form of therapy. According to the American Music Therapy Association, founded in 1998 as a merger between the National Association for Music Therapy and
10 the American Association for Music Therapy, music therapy can be defined as, "the clinical and evidence-based use of music interventions to accomplish individualized goals within a therapeutic

> dyslexics /dɪsˈleksɪks/ *n.* 诵读困难者
> *adj.* 诵读困难的
> merger /ˈmɜːdʒə/ *n.* (两个公司的)合并
> therapeutic /ˌθerəˈpjuːtɪk/ *adj.* 治疗(学)的；
> 疗法的；对身心健康有益的

relationship by a professional who has completed an approved music therapy program." This is
commonly used to treat everything from physical disabilities to chronic pain to brain injuries.

Even healthy people can be benefited through stress reduction or the use of music to aid in
childbirth. Nature and other environment sounds can also be therapeutic. Think of how relaxing the
sounds of a bubbling stream, crickets chirping, or ocean waves can be. Music therapy is considered
to be one of the "expressive therapies," others include art, dance, drama, play, writing, and humor
therapy.

Although the use of music to benefit health dates back to the days of Aristotle, modern music
therapy began shortly after World War II. Hospitals were hiring musicians to play for the
hospitalized veterans after seeing the good effect it had on those suffering from war-related mental
and emotional problems. Eventually colleges began to implement programs, and Michigan State
University began the world's first music therapy program in 1944.

There are many specific reasons why music therapy works. Music with a strong beat can
actually cause brainwaves to resonate in sync with the beat, with faster beats bringing sharper
concentration and more alert thinking, and a slower tempo promoting a calm, meditative state. This
can be good for you even after you stop listening, because it helps the brain in changing brainwave
speed by itself later.

Researchers at the University of Toronto are developing "brain wave music," a type of music therapy that involves creating music that imitates the patterns formed by individual brain waves. The people they test the music on are given their own CD, with music made for their specific brain waves. They're hoping that this new approach may help relieve chronic insomnia, anxiety, or depression, even without the additional aid (and risk of dependency) of medication. Could you imagine going to the doctors to get a "prescription CD?"

bubble /'bʌbəl/ *vt. & vi.* 起泡,使冒气泡 *n.* 水泡,气泡;泡影

cricket /'krɪkɪt/ *n.* 蟋蟀;板球

chirp /tʃɜːp/ *vi.* 鸟叫;虫鸣

Aristotle /'ærɪstɒtl/ *n.* 亚里士多德(古希腊大哲学家,科学家)

veteran /'vetərən/ *n.* 老兵;经验丰富的人

resonate /'rezəneɪt/ *vi.* 产生回声、共鸣或共振

sync /sɪŋk/ *n.* 同时;同步

tempo /'tempəʊ/ *n.* 〈意〉〈音〉乐曲的速度或拍子

meditative /'medɪtətɪv/ *adj.* 沉思的,冥想的

imitate /'ɪmɪteɪt/ *vt.* 模仿

chronic /'krɒnɪk/ *adj.* 长期患病的;慢性的

insomnia /ɪn'sɒmnɪə/ *n.* 〈医〉失眠(症)

93

In addition to causing positive changes in heart and breathing rates, bringing relaxation, and combating stress problems, music also brings a positive state of mind, helping to keep depression and anxiety at bay.

keep at bay 控制
obsess /əbˈses/ vt. 时刻困扰；缠住
intersect /ɪntəˈsekt/ vt. & vi. (指线条、道路等)相交，交叉
predate /ˈpriːdeɪt/ v. 居先；在日期上早于

Since music can do us so much good physically and mentally, we humans are obsessed with making all kinds of music which will comfort us, excite us, soothe us or even sadden us. Making music is one of our most basic instincts. There's a reason why we refer to music as the "universal language"; there has been no known human culture without music.

Dancing and music came before agriculture, and possibly even before language. Bone flutes were found in Europe dating back to 53,000 years ago. The head of the Biomusic program at the National Academy of the Sciences, Patricia Gray, and her colleagues comment, "The fact that whale and human music have so much in common even though our evolutionary paths have not intersected for 60 million years suggests that music may predate humans—that rather than being the inventors of music, we are latecomers to the musical scene."

READING COMPREHENSION

A **Choose the best answers for the following questions.**

1. Music can be used to treat many diseases EXCEPT _____.

    A. high blood pressure   B. reading difficulties

    C. old age   D. Alzheimer's disease

2. Even healthy people can be benefited through _____.

    A. stress reduction   B. the use of music to aid in childbirth

    C. relieving pain   D. both A and B

3. When did the modern music therapy begin?_____

    A. shortly after World War II   B. in the age of Aristotle

    C. in the 21th century   D. shortly after World War I

4. Making music is one of our most basic _____.

    A. abilities   B. instincts

    C. desires   D. requirements

5. Music comes before a lot things EXCEPT_____.

    A. argriculture   B. making instruments

    C. dancing   D. language

B **Answer the following questions.**

1. What is music used for in hospitals and nursing homes?

2. How can healthy people be benefited from music?

3. When did the use of music to benefit health date back to?

4. Why does music therapy work?

5. Which one came first, music or agriculture?

Unit 6

PART I   PREPARATORY

Read aloud the following sentences, paying attention to the meaning of the words in italics.

1. Strategically we should *despise* all our enemies.

2. He had to conceal his *identity* to escape the police.

3. They *adored* her as a living goddess.

4. There is no exactly *equivalent* French tense to the present perfect tense in English.

5. The fireman *demonstrated* great courage in saving the child.

6. The story will be continued in *subsequent* issues of the magazine.

7. He doesn't look like the usual *stereotype* of the city businessman with a dark suit.

8. They *proposed* to make arrangements beforehand.

9. The government would be unwise to *ignore* the growing dissatisfaction with its economic policies.

10. This is an *undeniable* fact.

WORDS LEARNED IN DISPLAY

Write the meaning of each of the following words in the corresponding blank. You can write either in English or in Chinese.

despise _____

identity _____

adore _____

equivalent _____

demonstrate _____

subsequent _____

stereotype _____

propose _____

ignore _____

undeniable _____

EXPRESSIONS IN CONTEXT

Study the following expressions and see how they are used in sentences.

take steps 采取措施,设法

◇ You must take steps to prevent it.

as far as...be concerned 就……而言

◇ As far as we're concerned you can go wherever you want.

in particular 尤其,特别

◇ I noticed his eyes in particular, because they were such an unusual color.

complain about 抱怨, 投诉

◇ He complained about the food.

take over 接管；接替

◇ The strikers took over the factories.

refer to...as 把……称作

◇ He had heard Evelyn refer to him as "Mattie."

as well as 也，又

◇ The conflict spread everywhere, into villages, as well as into the cities.

end in 以……为结果

◇ The argument between the two men ended in a fight.

EXPRESSIONS LEARNED IN DISPLAY

Complete each of the following sentences with the expressions you have just learned.

1. If you drive as recklessly as that, you'll _____ hospital.

2. Their full political rights, _____ their economic conditions, must be safeguarded.

3. The earlier the better,_____ the Committee _____.

4. He talked about sports in general and about football _____.

5. The speaker _____ him _____ an up-and-coming politician.

6. He never _____ working overtime.

7. People in that village _____ to improve their fire-fighting equipment.

8. We stop work at ten o'clock and the night shift _____ then.

PART II   LANGUAGE IN CONTEXT

GET YOURSELF INTERESTED

Read the following summary in Chinese and think what you are going to read in this text.

近年来在世界各地发起的"反全球化"运动提醒我们,在通往一个地球村的路上应该小心,不能失去每一个国家的传统文化特色。因为只有保留这些特色才能在全球化浪潮中维持那份珍贵的"多元化",世界才不致被"一律化"、"美国化"。

PREVIEW QUESTIONS

Work in pairs or groups and discuss the following questions.

1. How do you interpret "having no culture is a culture in itself"?

2. In what ways is the USA influencing the world?

3. Do you think the world is being Americanized? Why or why not?

READING SELECTION

Text A

How We Are Being Americanized

USA, which has the world's biggest economy and strongest known army, has taken gigantic steps in persuading the rest of the world to think and act like them. Many people, especially the Europeans, have often despised Americans saying they have no culture. But as any sociologist will tell you, even having no culture is a culture in itself. So for many years, the land of immigrants has been on a process of creating an identity and hence a culture. Now they seem to be selling their culture to the rest of the world as a new and improved product of what we all have as culture.

As far as fashion is concerned, the casual "American" style of wearing Jeans, T-Shirts and sports shoes is now common and acceptable in many places. For in the office it is not rare to see someone wearing tight jeans with a long sleeved shirt plus a tie. His defense is of course that it is the American style. Cowboy hats, boots and large silver belt buckles are also a common imitation of the dress style of Americans especially those from Texas and Arizona. Look at the music played in the Nyamirambo bound taxis and you will be amazed at how it matches with the dress style of the passengers!

Around the world the United States is perhaps best known for its numerous and successful fast food franchises. Such chains, including McDonald's, Burger King and Kentucky Fried Chicken are known for selling simply, pre-prepared food such as hamburgers, French fries (chips), soft drinks, fried chicken, and ice cream. Though undeniably popular, such food, with its emphasis on deep-frying, has been criticized by dietitians in recent decades for being unhealthy and a cause of obesity. It has thus become somewhat of a stereotype to associate American cuisine with obesity and junk food. The whole world now is full of similar eating joints. In Africa many are referred to as take-aways.

This transmission of American culture has been mainly through several conduits with the

gigantic /dʒaɪˈɡæntɪk/ *adj.* 巨大的，庞大的

despise /dɪˈspaɪz/ *vt.* 鄙视，看不起某人(某事)

sociologist /ˌsəʊsɪˈɒlədʒɪst/ *n.* 社会学家

immigrant /ˈɪmɪɡrənt/ *n.* 移民

sleeved /sliːvd/ *adj.* 有袖子的

buckle /ˈbʌkəl/ *n.* 搭扣，扣环

imitation /ˌɪmɪˈteɪʃn/ *n.* 模仿，仿效；仿制品，伪造物

numerous /ˈnjuːmərəs/ *adj.* 很多的，许多的

franchise /ˈfræntʃaɪz/ *n.* 特许经营，特许权，专营权

undeniable /ˌʌndɪˈnaɪəbəl/ *adj.* 不可否认的

dietitian /ˌdaɪəˈtɪʃən/ *n.* 饮食学家，营养学家，膳食学家

obesity /əʊˈbiːsɪti/ *n.* 肥胖，肥大

stereotype /ˈstɪərɪətaɪp/ *n.* 老套，模式化的见解，成见

cuisine /kwɪˈziːn/ *n.* 烹饪艺术，菜肴

junk food *n.* 垃圾食品，无营养食品

eating joint 〈美俚〉小饭馆

transmission /trænzˈmɪʃən/ *n.* 传送，传播，传达

conduit /ˈkɑːnduɪt/ *n.* 管道，渠道

30 number one medium being the electronic media. Television in particular has done a lot in Americanizing those who view images especially from Hollywood. The guys in Hollywood have made us to adore the tough cigar-smoking guys in the casinos, the thin-shapely long-legged women, and to dream about rags-to-riches stories that are a common tag line of the movies. We now adore jazz, hip-hop, rap music, country music as well as gospel music, all of which were
35 pioneered by the United States.

And trust us in following the Uncle Sam; many countries now have equivalents of the American awards of Oscars for the movies and Grammy's for the music. Just check out the PAM awards in Uganda or the Kisima awards in Kenya, not forgetting the continental Kora awards held annually in South Africa. Many countries have also gone ahead to construct
40 theme parks based on the American Disney World model. Americanization has also led to the popularity and acceptability of what is known as American English. I have seen many posters here in Rwanda of schools claiming to teach American English. Many youths are now using this type of English considering it "modern".

We ought not to ignore the heavy influence that the United States has demonstrated in the
45 development of the Internet and its subsequent control. Remember the conference that was held at the beginning of this year in Tunisia where nations were complaining about the control the US has over the Internet. They
50 were proposing that instead an international body should take over but the conference ended in defeat of this line of argument. The iPod, the most popular gadget for portable digital music, is also an American invention.
55 The number one medium for the transmission of American culture has been through electronic media, television in particular.

electronic media 电子宣传工具(指广播、电视)

adore /ə'dɔː/ vt. 爱慕，崇拜

casino /kə'siːnəʊ/ n. 赌场，娱乐场

jazz /dʒæz/ n. 爵士乐

hip-hop n. 嘻哈

rap /ræp/ n. 说唱

equivalent /ɪ'kwɪvələnt/ n. 同等物，等价物，相等物

continental /ˌkɒntɪ'nentəl/ adj. 大陆的，大陆性的，欧洲大陆的

annually /'ænjʊəli/ adv. 一年一次，每年

theme park n. (游乐园中的)主题乐园

acceptability /əkˌseptə'bɪlɪti/ n. 可接受性

demonstrate /'demənstreɪt/ vi. 显示，表露

subsequent /'sʌbsɪkwənt/ adj. 随后的，继……之后的

propose /prə'pəʊz/ vt. & vi. 提议，建议

iPod 音乐播放器

gadget /'gædʒɪt/ n. 小机械，小器具

portable /'pɔːtəbəl/ adj. 便于携带的，手提式的，轻便的

digital /'dɪdʒɪtl/ adj. 数字式的，数码的，数字显示的

American sports, especially basketball, have now become famous worldwide, especially among college students. However, other games like baseball and American football have not been easily adopted by other people in the world, as has been the case with basketball. Soccer, which is known to be the world's most popular sport, is not so popular in the US. However, the US women's soccer team is one of the world's premier women's sides.

premier /'premiə/ *adj.* 最好的，最重要的

COMPREHENSION CHECK

Understanding the General Ideas

Discuss the following questions in pairs or groups. The key words given in the brackets may help you in your discussion.

1. How do you interpret many people's opinion that Americans have no culture?

   (immigrants, identity, culture)

2. What is the author's attitude toward the opinion that Americans have no culture?

   (positive, negative, agree, disagree)

3. According to the author, how are we being Americanized?

   (fashion, food, media, sports, etc.)

4. How does the author develop his topic?

   (inductive, deductive, reductive)

5. In your opinion, are we being Americanized? Why or why not?

   (yes, no)

Understanding the Specifics

Read the following sentences and tell if they are true or false according to the text. In the brackets leading each statement, put "T" for true or "F" for false.

1. (   ) USA is a land of immigrants without a culture in itself.

2. (   ) The casual "American" style of wearing Jeans, T-shirts and sports shoes is now acceptable even in the office.

3. (   ) All the food sold in McDonald's, Burger King and Kentucky Fried Chicken is deep-fried and unhealthy.

4. (   ) The electronic media play a crucial role in transmitting American culture.

5. (   ) The underlined phrase "the Uncle Sam" in the 5th paragraph refers to the USA.

6. (   ) Like the iPod, the Disney World is also an American invention.

7. (   ) After the conference in Tunisia an international body took over the control over the Internet.

8. (   ) Baseball and American football are popular only in the USA.

STUDY AND PRACTICE

Vocabulary

Fill in the blanks with the words below. Change the form where necessary.

numerous	transmission	equivalent (*n.*)	demonstrate
propose	premier (*adj.*)	adore	despise
stereotype (*n.*)	undeniable		

1. Marcel _____ her; and what would he do without her?

2. There are _____ people in the square.

3. Honest boys _____ lies and liars.

4. She believes that she is not a good mother because she does not fit the _____ of a woman who spends all her time with her children.

5. She attends Britain's _____ university.

6. It's _____ that she is the best person for the job.

7. We interrupt our normal _____ to bring you a piece of special news.

8. Recent events _____ the need for a change in policy.

9. The vitamin pill is the _____ of three eggs and a glass of milk.

10. I wish to _____ a toast to our friendship.

Expressions

Rewrite the following sentences with the help of the phrases and expressions provided. The italicized part in each sentence may serve as the hint for your task. The first sentence is done for you.

take steps	as far as...be concerned	in particular	complain about
take over	refer to... as	as well as	end in

1. *In my opinion,* the whole idea is crazy.

   As far as I'm concerned, the whole idea is crazy.

2. I'm feeling too tired to drive any more; will you *drive the car instead of me*?

   _____

3. Their marriage *was brought to a close in* divorce.

_____

4. Bacteriology, *especially* microbiology, had fascinated him from his earliest student days.

_____

5. The scientist *spoke about* the discovery as the most exciting new development in this field.

_____

6. We saw a Mickey Mouse cartoon *in addition to* the cowboy movie.

_____

7. We must *take action* to help the families of those who were hurt.

_____

8. They *expressed bitter feelings over* the injustice of the system.

_____

Translation

A From Chinese to English

1. 没人会瞧不起你。

2. 你必须采取措施减少开支。

3. 我提议休息半小时。

4. 一些美国英语在英国英语中没有对应的词语。

5. 这部电影中的人物只是一些丝毫没有个性的俗套人物。

6. 我们原计划去游览,但后来汽车出了故障,没有去成。

7. 我们的邻居说,我们如果再吵闹,他就要向警方投诉我们了。

8. 他不喜欢我,所以我们见面时他没理我。

B From English to Chinese

1. USA, which has the world's biggest economy and strongest known army, has taken gigantic steps in persuading the rest of the world to think and act like them.

2. Though undeniably popular, such food, with its emphasis on deep-frying, has been criticized by dietitians in recent decades for being unhealthy and a cause of obesity.

3. The guys in Hollywood have made us to adore the tough cigar-smoking guys in the casinos, the thin-shapely long-legged women, and to dream about rags-to-riches stories that are a common tag line of the movies.

4. We ought not to ignore the heavy influence that the United States has demonstrated in the development of the Internet and its subsequent control.

5. However, other games like baseball and American football have not been easily adopted by other people in the world, as has been the case with basketball.

GRAMMAR

Passive Voice (被动语态) (I)

1. 主动语态与被动语态

1) 基本概念

主语和谓语有时是主动关系,即主语是动作的执行者,如:

Everybody respects him.

有时也可以是被动关系,及主语是动作的承受者,如:

He is respected by everybody.

第一句的谓语为主动语态,第二句的谓语为被动语态。这里也可以看出被动结构中的主语是主动结构句子中的宾语,主动结构中的主语在被动结构中由介词 by 引导,并在句中充当状语。当然,并不是每一个被动结构都有由 by 引导的状语,如:

They were given a warm welcome.

She was born in Hunan Province.

由此可以看出,被动语态是由"be+V-ed 分词"构成。 一般时态的被动语态如下:

You are invited to give us a talk in English.

They were given a warm send-off at the airport.

The spacecraft will be launched tomorrow.

I didn't expect that I would be asked to speak.

They are being questioned by the police.

The troops were being inspected by the president.

They have been warned not to swim there.

He told me that the factory had been closed down.

2) 可变为被动语态的动词

(1) 一般说来,及物动词可用于被动语态:

主动结构	被动结构
He writes many letters every day.	Many letters are written every day.
They import a great deal of rice.	A great deal of rice is imported.

(2) 不及物动词若与介词结合可用于被动语态:

主动结构	被动结构
We are looking into the case.	The case is being looked into.
He operated on her yesterday.	She was operated on yesterday.

(3) 由情态动词等构成的谓语也可用于被动结构:

主动结构	被动结构
We can't do it in a day.	It can't be done in a day.
You must do it right now.	It must be done right now.

(4) 非限定动词,由于不是谓语,不能改为被动语态,但可改为被动形式:

主动形式	被动形式
She asked to see the manager.	She asked to be given a job.
I have nothing to do.	There is nothing to be done.

3) 可变为被动结构的结构

除了"主+谓+宾"这种结构可变为被动结构外,还有以下结构可变为被动结构:

(1) 主语+谓语+宾语+不定式

主动结构	被动结构
We told the boy to go to bed.	The boy was told to go to bed.
They asked her to sing a song.	She was asked to sing a song.

(2) 主语+谓语+宾语+名词作补语

主动结构	被动结构
They made him their leader.	He was made their leader.
We called her Big Sister.	She was called Big Sister.

(3) 主语+谓语+宾语+形容词作补语

主动结构	被动结构
She painted the walls yellow.	The walls were painted yellow.
They set her free.	She was set free.

(4) 主语+谓语+间接宾语+直接宾语(+其他部分)

主动结构	被动结构
They gave me something to eat.	I was given something to eat.
	Something was given to me to eat.
She taught me an English song.	I was taught an English song.
	An English song was taught to me.

(5) 主语+谓语+从句

主动结构	被动结构
They said that she was a saint.	It was said that she was a saint.
They believe that he has magic power.	It's believed that he has magic power.

2. 被动结构的使用场合

1）不知道动作的执行者是谁，这时只好用被动结构：

Three people were injured.

The building was burned down.

The boy was nearly drowned.

2）不必提到动作的执行者，因此也可用被动结构：

The book was published in 2000.

The plant was shut down for two months.

3）动作的承受者（或结果）是谈话的中心：

Are these goods made by machinery?

These motions can be vetoed by the Governor.

4）动作的执行者很模糊（如 people, one 等），故用被动结构也很自然：

It's suggested that we put the meeting off.

The letter has been opened.

5）为了措辞上的缘故，常避免说出动作的执行者：

You are requested to give us a talk on Japanese culture.

It is generally considered rude to stare at people.

6）为了使句子得到更好的安排：

He appeared on the stage and was warmly applauded by the audience.

The plan was supported by those who wish to live on the campus.

IMMEDIATE PRACTICE

Fill in the blanks with appropriate forms of the words given.

1. A new library _____ (build) in our city now.

2. We shall _____ (ask) to attend the meeting.

3. He has worked in the factory since it _____ (build) 10 years ago.

4. So far, many man-made satellites _____ (send) up into space.

5. Sheep _____ (keep) by farmers to _____ (produce) wool and mutton.

6. Outer space _____ (not explore) by people before 1957.

7. Computer science _____ (teach) now almost in all universities and institutes.

8. The first railway in the world _____ (design) in the last century.

9. Five units of this textbook _____ (study) by the end of last month.

10. A beautiful horse _____ (draw) by John tomorrow.

Translate the following sentences into English.

1. 这三个单词发音相同。

2. 这本小说是路遥写的。

3. 这项工程什么时候完工?

4. 她没想到会受到邀请。

5. 这案子正在调查之中。

6. 这些古建筑正在翻修。

7. 还没告诉她这件事。

8. 我听说她已被送进医院。

9. 这不是短期内能完成的。

10. 玻璃器皿必须轻拿轻放。

PART III   TOWARD PRODUCTIVE LANGUAGE

READING ACTIVITIES

Read the following very quickly and try to get the general meaning; do not worry if you come across some new words.

全球化是个客观的历史进程,它所描述的是世界作为一个整体的发展,带来的结果则是涉及全球范围的深刻变革,即使上个世纪90年代之后来势凶猛的全球化在许多方面打上了美国的烙印,但这种性质不会发生根本改变。美国化只是局限于美国大众文化向外传播对全球发生的一种影响,它在一定的时空范围会导致被影响国的文化发生方向的改变,但不会使他们完全丧失自我认同,从根本上趋同于美国文化。

Text B

Americanization or Globalization

Global sociopolitical issues never cease to fascinate any interested soul.   From the times of civilization came the era of colonialism and then independence.   This was followed by the cold war era.   The post cold war era led to the increasing influence of what some people these days call quasi-

5 governments (such as the International Monetary Fund and the World Bank).

The IMF and the World Bank consequently took on the role of the world's economic "police" telling particularly poorer nations how to spend their money.

10 In order to receive more aid,   these Bretton Woods

globalization /ɡləʊbəlaɪˈzeɪʃən/ *n.* 全球化,全球性

sociopolitical /ˌsəʊsɪəʊpəˈlɪtɪkəl/ *adj.* 社会政治的,同时涉及社会和政治的

fascinate /ˈfæsɪneɪt/ *vt.* 使着迷,使极感兴趣

colonialism /kəˈləʊnɪəlɪzəm/ *n.* 殖民主义,殖民政策

quasi /ˈkweɪzaɪ,ˈkwɑːzɪ/ *adj.* 类似的,准的

International Monetary Fund *n.* 国际货币基金会

World Bank *n.* 世界银行

consequently /ˈkɒnsɪkwəntlɪ/ *adv.* 所以,因此

Institutions demanded that countries open up their economies to liberalization under Structural Adjustment Programmes that encouraged governments to fund privatization programmes, ahead of welfare and public services. Concurrently we had the influence of multinational organizations like the United Nations Organization also greatly formatting global issues.

15　　　Fast-forward to the new millennium things took a different path. All of a sudden we were being pumped with the rhetoric titled globalization. Globalization is an umbrella term for a complex series of economic, social, technological, and political changes seen as increasing interdependence and interaction between people and companies in disparate locations. In general use within the field of economics and political economy, it refers to the increasing integration of economies 20 around the world, particularly through trade and financial flows. The term sometimes also refers to the movement of people (labor) and knowledge (technology) across international borders. There are also broader cultural, political and environmental dimensions of globalization. For the common man it was always argued that the world had become like a global village of sorts.

　　　At its most basic, there is nothing 25 mysterious about globalization. Howewever, some people are now arguing that globalization has mainly benefited the already strong economies of the world and it has given them leverage to not only trade with the rest of the 30 world but to also influence their general lifestyles and politics. Proponents of this school of thought contend that countries like U.S.A. are using the globalization as an engine of "corporate imperialism," one which tramples 35 over the human rights of developing societies, claims to bring prosperity, yet often simply amounts to plundering and profiteering.

　　　Another negative effect of globalization

Bretton Woods Institutions　布雷顿森林机构，指 IMF 和世界银行

liberalization /ˌlɪbərəlaɪzeɪʃən/ n. 自由主义化，使宽大

privatization /praɪvɪtaɪˈzeɪʃən/ n. 私有化，私人化

welfare /ˈwelfeə/ n. 繁荣；福利

concurrently /kənˈkʌrəntlɪ/ adv. 同时存在(发生、完成)

multinational /mʌltɪˈnæʃənəl/ adj. 多国的

format /ˈfɔːmæt/ v. 安排，计划

rhetoric /ˈretərɪk/ n. 雄辩言辞，虚夸的言辞

disparate /ˈdɪspərət/ adj. 根本不同的，不能相比较的

integration /ˌɪntɪˈgreɪʃən/ n. 结合，整合，一体化

financial flow　资金流量

dimension /daɪˈmenʃən/ n. 维度，规模，程度

leverage /ˈliːvərɪdʒ/ n. 力量，影响

proponent /prəˈpəʊnənt/ n. 支持者，拥护者

corporate /ˈkɔːpərət/ adj. 企业的，法人的

imperialism /ɪmˈpɪərɪəlɪzəm/ n. 帝国主义，帝国主义政策

trample /ˈtræmpəl/ vt. & vi. 踩，踏

plunder /ˈplʌndə/ vt. & vi. 掠夺；抢劫

profiteering /prɒfiˈtɪərɪŋ/ n. 暴利，不正当利益

has been cultural assimilation via cultural imperialism. This can be further explained as a
40 situation of exporting of artificial wants, and the destruction or inhibition of authentic local
cultures. At a closer look, globalization is slowly shifting towards Americanization. Have you
heard the word "Americanization"? Well in the early 1900's Americanization meant taking new
immigrants and turning them into Americans—whether they wanted to give up their traditional
ways or not. This process often involved learning English and adjusting to American culture,
45 customs, and dress.

Critics now say globalization is nothing more than the imposition of American culture on
the entire world. In fact, the most visible sign of globalization seems to be the spread of American
hamburgers and cola (Pepsi and Coca Cola products) to nearly every country on earth. The song
"Amerika" by the German rock band Rammstein is often seen as a satire of Americanization. It
50 has received mixed reviews: some perceive it as anti-American, others as being opposed to
globalization. The band views it as a satirical commentary on "cocacolonization."

In an article discussing why terrorists hate the United States, The New York *Times* columnist
Thomas Friedman wrote: "...globalization is in so many ways Americanization: globalization wears
Mickey Mouse ears, it drinks Pepsi and Coke, eats Big Macs, does its computing on an IBM
55 laptop with Windows 98. Many societies around
the world can't get enough of it, but others see
it as a fundamental threat."

The rest of the world seems to be following
Uncle Sam (U.S.A.) and leaving behind its
60 authentic ways of life. Americanization is the
contemporary term used for the influence the
United States of America has on the culture of
other countries, substituting their culture with
American culture. When encountered unwillingly,
65 it has a negative connotation; when sought
voluntarily, it has a positive connotation.

assimilation /əsɪmɪˈleɪʃən/ *n.* (被)吸收或同化的过程
via /ˈvaɪə/ *prep.* 经由,经过
artificial /ˌɑːtɪˈfɪʃəl/ *adj.* 人造的,人工的;假的
inhibition /ɪnhɪˈbɪʃən/ *n.* 抑制
authentic /ɔːˈθentɪk/ *adj.* 真的,真正的
adjust to 调整,调节,适应
satire /ˈsætaɪə/ *n.* 讽刺,讥讽,讽刺作品
commentary /ˈkɒməntərɪ/ *n.* 实况报道;评论
terrorist /ˈterərɪst/ *n.* 恐怖主义者,恐怖分子
laptop /ˈlæptɒp/ *n.* 便携式电脑
contemporary /kənˈtempərərɪ/ *adj.* 当代的;同时代的
substitute /ˈsʌbstɪtjuːt/ *vt. & vi.* 代替,替换
connotation /kɒnəˈteɪʃən/ *n.* 内涵意义,隐含意义

A Choose the best answers for the following questions.

1. The author mentions IMF and the World Bank to show _____.

   A. that they took on the role of the world's economic "police"

   B. that they are Bretton Woods institutions

   C. that they are helping poorer nations to open up their economies

   D. that they are more and more influential in global issues in the post cold war era

2. The phrase "of sorts" in the 4th paragraph most probably means _____.

   A. of an unusual kind   B. of a poor or doubtful kind

   C. in some way or degree   D. rather

3. According to the text, all the following statements about globalization are ture EXCEPT

   _____.

   A. Generally speaking, it is used within the field of economics and political economy to refer

   to the increasing integration of economies around the world.

   B. It is sometimes used to refer to the movement of people and knowledge across international

   borders.

   C. It is used for a complex series of economic, social, technological and political changes.

   D. People and companies in different places are more and more independent of each

   other.

4. The phrase "nothing more than" in the 7th paragraph most probably means_____.

   A. only   B. mere   C. except   D. frequently

5. In Thomas Friedman's opinion, terrorists hate the United States probably because _____.

   A. they think they should get enough American products

   B. they can't get enough of globalization

C. they think globalization is a fundamental threat because it is in so many ways Americanization

D. they can't get enough of Americanization

B Answer the following questions.

1. What do you know about IMF and the World Bank? Do you know the Bretton Woods Conference and the Bretton Woods System?

2. What does the author mean by "globalization"? What do you know about globalization?

3. In the author's opinion, what are the negative effects of globalization?

4. What is the author's attitude toward Americanization?

5. What's your attitude toward Americanization and globalization?

Unit 7

WORDS IN CONTEXT

Read aloud the following sentences, paying attention to the meaning of the words in italics.

1. Both of them were of good *character* and they seemed compatible together.

2. Lisa moved to a city near Hollywood to *pursue* her acting career.

3. As a *token* of our thanks for all that you have done, we would like you to accept this small gift.

4. Nixon was the first US president to *resign* before the end of his term of office.

5. In spring, I shall plant a tree to the memory of my *beloved* friend.

6. Still holding her hand, he suddenly became aware that it was a *privilege* that she had allowed him to accompany her while she was passing away peacefully.

7. Self-respect and a clear conscience are powerful components of *integrity* and are the basis for enriching your relationships with others.

8. Our ultimate *objective* is to have as many female members of parliament as there are male.

9. *Virtuous* persons may be considered fortunate if their virtue is recognized and publicly applauded.

10. We must have the right to carry out our duty to *impart* the moral convictions and knowledge to our own children.

WORDS AND PHRASES LEARNED IN DISPLAY

Write the meaning of each of the following words in the corresponding blank. You can write either in English or in Chinese.

character _____

pursue _____

token _____

resign _____

beloved _____

privilege _____

integrity _____

objective _____

virtuous _____

impart _____

EXPRESSIONS IN CONTEXT

Study the following expressions and see how they are used in sentences.

pray for 祈祷,祷祝,祈求

◇ We observed Memorial Day by going to church and praying for the dead.

dedicate oneself to 专心致力于

◇ Proper steps should be taken to encourage people to dedicate their whole lives to education.

be obliged to 不得不

◇ If you cannot deliver the goods on time, I shall be obliged to send you to court.

stick to 坚持

◇ Everyone should stick to his words.

be limited in 受限制的,有限的

◇ Natural gas, the purest of the three fuels, is also the most limited in supply.

make use of 利用,使用

◇ We had better make use of something inexpensive.

at large 一般来说;普遍

◇ People at large approve of the new policy.

contribute to 捐献,贡献

◇ His speech has contributed to the widespread adoption and acceptance of the new law.

EXPRESSIONS LEARNED IN DISPLAY

Complete each of the following sentences with the expressions you have just learned.

1. I sat in church and wanted to ask the priest to _____ the people with AIDS in Zimbabwe and all over the world.

2. The new president said she would _____ protecting the rights of the old, the sick and the homeless.

3. Peter had never shown the slightest interest in his job, so I did not feel _____ give him a good reference.

4. It would only weaken his position if he continues to _____ his strange ideas.

5. He ran away twice from his boarding school because he couldn't put up with _____ an institution.

6. Students should be conscious of the value of knowledge and try their best to _____ their university life.

7. In the hot season there is not much variation of temperature _____.

8. The arrangement will _____ cementing our pleasant relationship.

PART II   LANGUAGE IN CONTEXT

Read the following summary in Chinese and think what you are going to read in this text.

> 孔子是中国古代最有影响的哲学家。虽然他自称"述而不作",而实际上他在诸子百家争鸣之前夕,开创性地建立了一个包括天道观、人道观、认识论、方法论等方面的哲学思想体系。其学说内涵丰富,自成系统,在中国历史上产生了深远的影响。了解孔子坎坷的人生,寻找伟大思想迸发的源泉!

PREVIEW QUESTIONS

Work in pairs or groups and discuss the following questions.

1. Do you know Confucius? Where did you get the information?

2. Have you read *The Analects of Confucius*? What do you think of this book?

3. Do you think Confucius' ideas are still very useful to people nowadays?

READING SELECTION

Text A

Confucius

Confucius has proved to be the greatest influence over the Chinese character. Besides being a great educationist, thinker and unsuccessful politician, he was first of all an intellect with a noble morality. He pursued truth, kindness and perfection throughout his life and his success and failure were largely due to his character, which had an everlasting impact on Chinese intellect.

Confucius was born in 551 B.C. in the State of Lu known today as Qufu in Shandong Province. In Chinese, his name was Kong Qiu. This was because his parents had prayed for a son at Niqiu Hill and "Qiu" was an appropriate token of their thanks and joy at having their prayers answered. Sadly, his father died when Confucius was very young but despite a hard life, Confucius dedicated himself to study at the age of 15.

Patriotism was the driving force for young Confucius and he set his sights on an official career as a means to apply his political ideals. He had gained some fame by the time he was 30 but it was not until he was 51 that his official life really assumed great importance. This eventful career was to last for only four years as he was forced to resign when he found it impossible to agree with the authorities. Such was the opposition to his ideas that he was obliged to leave his country and to travel around the states. During these 14 years, he was in danger on many occasions and even risked his life. At the age of 68 he was welcomed back to Lu but he was set up as a respected gentleman without any authority. He died of illness at the age of 73. A brilliant star fell into silence. His students treated him as father and wore the willow for three years. Zigong, one of the famous disciples, set up a cabinet near his tomb and stayed there for six years to mourn his beloved teacher. Confucius could never have dreamed that his lonely tomb would develop into the large Cemetery of Confucius and that his ideological system would become the norm for Chinese society.

Compared to his frustrated political career, Confucius' career as a teacher and philosopher was brilliant and full of achievements.

character /'kærɪktə/ n. 特征,性质,性格
educationist /,edjʊ'keɪʃənɪst/ n. 教育家
intellect /'ɪntəlekt/ n. 文人,知识分子
morality /mə'rælɪtɪ/ n. 道德
pursue /pə'sjuː/ vt. 追求,从事
perfection /pə'fekʃən/ n. 完美,完善
everlasting /,evə'lɑːstɪŋ/ adj. 永恒的,持久的
pray for 请求,恳求
token /'təʊkən/ n. 表征,记号
dedicate oneself to 专心致力于
patriotism /'pætrɪətɪzəm/ n. 爱国心,爱国精神
ideal /aɪ'dɪəl/ n. 理想
eventful /ɪ'ventfəl/ adj. 充满大事的,重大的
resign /rɪ'zaɪn/ v. 辞去,辞职
be obliged to 不得不
authority /ɔː'θɒrɪtɪ/ n. 权力,当权的地位;当权者;[复数]当局,官方
wear the willow 悲悼心爱者的去世
disciple /dɪ'saɪpəl/ n. 弟子,门徒
cabinet /'kæbɪnɪt/ n. 小屋;橱柜
beloved /bɪ'lʌvɪd/ adj. 敬爱的
cemetery /'semɪtrɪ/ n. 墓地,公墓
ideological /,aɪdɪə'lɒdʒɪkəl/ adj. 意识形态的

120

Much of his approach to education was avante garde as he promoted the ideas "to educate all despite their social status" and "to teach according to the students' characteristics." The first of these broke with tradition as only the aristocracy had the privilege of education.

Confucius also proposed a complete set of principles concerning study. He said, "Studying without thinking leads to confusion; thinking without studying leads to laziness." Today's quality-education was nothing new to Confucius.

Imparting knowledge was only part of his teaching; he was a living example of the concepts he promoted and this had a deep and lasting influence upon his disciples. Confucius' private life was a model of his doctrines. *The Analects of Confucius* provides a vivid record of his teachings. Although he wrote nothing personally, his words were collected and recorded for posterity by his disciples. The accumulated words of wisdom have come down to us as "The Analects," one of the most important of all the Chinese classics.

Confucius took great delight in studying and was modest enough to learn from anyone else. He was never tired of teaching his disciples and his unremitting pursuit of truth, ideas and perfect personality, his integrity, kindness, modesty and courteousness deeply inspired his disciples and the intellects of subsequent generations. Uniquely, only he is qualified to be called "the teacher of ten thousand generations." It is said that among 3,000 of Confucius' disciples, there were 72 who were brilliant and who succeeded in morality, literature, language, and especially politics. These brilliant disciples contributed much to the spreading, formation and development of Confucianism.

Confucius stuck to righteousness, saying, "Improper fortunes are just flowing clouds to me. For proper fortunes, I will do jobs such as a driver." He was quite easy with his ideas despite of poverty. He was virtuous, always ready to help others and treated others with tolerance and honesty. To him, a benevolent person is one who

avante garde /ˌævɒŋˈɡɑːd/ (法) 前卫
aristocracy /ˌærɪˈstɒkrəsɪ/ *n.* 贵族, 贵族政权
privilege /ˈprɪvɪlɪdʒ/ *n.* 特权
impart /ɪmˈpɑːt/ *v.* 传授
doctrine /ˈdɒktrɪn/ *n.* 教条, 学说
analects /ˈænəlekts/ *n.* [复]文选, 论集
posterity /pɒsˈterɪtɪ/ *n.* 子孙, 后代
unremitting /ˌʌnrɪˈmɪtɪŋ/ *adj.* 不懈的
integrity /ɪnˈtegrɪtɪ/ *n.* 正直, 诚实
contribute to 捐献, 贡献
stick to 坚持
righteousness /ˈraɪtʃəsnɪs/ *n.* 正当, 正义, 正直
virtuous /ˈvɜːtʃʊəs/ *adj.* 善良的, 有道德的
benevolent /bɪˈnevələnt/ *adj.* 慈善的

loves others. He said, "Do not give others what you do
60　not want yourself," similar to the *Bible* teaching of "All
those things which you would have men do to you, even
so do you to them: because this is the law and the
prophets."

prophet /ˈprɒfit/ *n.* 先知,预言者
be limited in 限制于
objective /əbˈdʒektɪv/ *n.* 目的,目标
make use of 利用,使用
at large 一般来说;普遍;充分地,全面地

　　Influenced by Confucianism, in Chinese culture, an intellectual is not limited in study alone.
65　He should be successful in being a human and in his bearing of himself. A key objective of an
intellectual should be to make full use of his ability, personality and intelligence to do good for
the state, society and the world at large.

COMPREHENSION CHECK

Understanding the General Ideas

*Discuss the following questions in pairs or groups. The key words given in the brackets may
help you in your discussion.*

　1. What influenced the Chinese intellects greatly according to the passage?

　　(character, truth, kindness)

2. Why was Confucius named Kong Qiu?

　　(expectation, Niqiu, token)

3. Why did Confucius want to pursue an official position in his youth?

　　(love his country, the state and the society, driving force)

4. Can you list some principles proposed by Confucius concerning study?

　　(educate, social status, the students' characteristics)

5. Had Confucius collected and recorded his statements and published them as *Analects of
Confucius?*

　　(his disciples, collect, record)

Understanding the Specifics

Read the following sentences and tell if they are true or false according to the text. In the brackets leading each statement, put "T" for true or "F" for false.

1. (   ) Confucius had gained great fame in his early age.

2. (   ) Much of Confucius' approach to education was avante garde.

3. (   ) Confucius never came back to his motherland Lu after he left his country to travel around the states.

4. (   ) Zigong could never have dreamed that his ideological system would become the norm for Chinese society.

5. (   ) Confucius had a good relationship with the authorities.

6. (   ) *The Analects of Confucius* provides a vivid record of his teachings.

7. (   ) Confucius died of illness at the age of 84.

8. (   ) Confucius is the only person who proposed a complete set of principles concerning study in Chinese history.

STUDY AND PRACTICE

Vocabulary

Fill in the blanks with the words below. Change the form where necessary.

impact	resign	token	doctrine	virtuous
pursue	privilege	impart	objective	beloved

1. My choice is to _____ happiness by serving the community with my knowledge and

hard work.

2. The general _____ of the group is to promote student involvement in their residential

communities.

3. The consequences of the Industrial Revolution had a major _____ on much of America

in the 20th century.

4. What bothers the writer is that some of the boy's teachers weren't happy with the _____

reward for his good deed.

5. I had the _____ of playing alongside him in his farewell match.

6. A _____ person is an honorable person, a person who ought to be honored by the

community in which he or she lives.

7. It is a pleasant prospect for Jim to marry his _____ girlfriend and live a happy family life.

8. Christianity continued to uphold the _____ of the one god as creator of the universe.

9. The news that the Director was to _____ threw the company into confusion.

10. One big difference between humans and animals is that animals cannot _____

experience to their offspring.

Expressions

Rewrite the following sentences with the help of the phrases and expressions provided. The italicized part in each sentence may serve as the hint for your task. The first sentence is done for you.

pray for	**dedicate oneself to**	**stick to**	**be limited in**
at large	**make use of**	**contribute to**	**be obliged to**

1. I hope the new measures will *be good for* preventing inflation in the price of housing.

   I hope the new measures will *contribute to* preventing inflation in the price of housing.

2. The new president said she would *devote herself to* protecting the rights of the old, the sick

and the homeless.

_____

3. Students should be conscious of the value of knowledge and try their best to *take advantage of* their university life.

_____

4. It would only weaken his position if he continues to *adhere to* his strange ideas.

_____

5. Elementary education is an important issue that needs to be discussed by society *at utmost.*

_____

6. If you don't drive carefully, I shall *be forced to* deprive you of your license.

_____

7. The people in church last Sunday *knelt down to ask God* to help the hungry.

_____

8. He ran away twice from his boarding school because he couldn't put up with *being restricted in* an institution.

_____

Translation

A From Chinese to English

1. 孔子十五志于学。

2. 学而不思则罔,思而不学则殆。

3. 有教无类,因材施教。

4. 许多科学家都把自己的身心贡献给了国家。

5. 多谢您为这项基金做了慷慨的捐赠。

6. 我没有什么重要的事情给你们传达。

7.《论语》是由孔子的弟子收集编纂而成。

8. 在孔子时代,接受教育是贵族的一种特权。

B From English to Chinese

1. Patriotism was the driving force for young Confucius and he set his sights on an official career as a means to apply his political ideals.

2. Confucius could never have dreamed that his lonely tomb would develop into the large Cemetery of Confucius and that his ideological system would become the norm for Chinese society.

3. Imparting knowledge was only part of his teaching; he was a living example of the concepts he promoted and this had a deep and lasting influence upon his disciples.

4. A key objective of an intellectual should be to make full use of his ability, personality and intelligence to do good for the state, society and the world at large.

5. Influenced by Confucianism, in Chinese culture, an intellectual is not limited in study alone.

GRAMMAR

Passive Voice (被动语态) (II)

3. 非谓语动词的被动形式

1) 不定式的被动形式

(1) 用作宾语

I must ask to be excused.

(2) 构成复合宾语

She didn't want her son to be taken away.

(3) 用作定语

She was invited to a party to be held that night.

(4) 用作状语

They were shipped to America to be sold as slaves.

(5) 用作主语

It's an honor to be invited to the ceremony.

(6) 用作表语

My only wish is to be allowed to try my method.

2) V-ing 的被动形式

(1) 构成复合宾语

I saw him being carried away on a stretcher.

(2) 用作定语

She was not interested in the question being discussed.

(3) 用作状语

Being protected by a thick wall, they felt quite safe.

(4) 用作动词宾语或介词宾语

He hated being laughed at.

He was far from being satisfied.

(5) 用作主语

Being offered such a job was sheer good luck.

4. 英汉被动语态的用法比较

1) 英汉被动意义表示法比较

英语动词的被动语态是由 be+ -ed 分词构成的;汉语动词无词形变化,被动意义只能通过一定的词汇形式来表示,如:

John was elected monitor.　　　　约翰当选为班长。

This young worker should be praised in the whole factory.

这位青年工人应受到全厂表扬。

2) 英汉主动结构表示被动意义

英语中有些动词能以主动语态表示被动意义,这种情况在汉语中能以相应的形式表示,如:

This piece of cloth has worn thin.　　　　这块布磨薄了。

Mind your hat, it'll blow into the river.　　　　当心你的帽子吹到河里去。

Tomatoes bruise easily.　　　　西红柿很容易碰伤。

My voice doesn't carry well.　　　　我的声音传不远。

The match lights easily.　　　　这火柴很容易划着。

反之,汉语中出现这种情况时,英语未必都有相应的形式,往往还是要采用被动语态,如:

这个问题明天上午讨论吗?　　　　Will the question be discussed tomorrow morning?

这件事马上可以做。　　　　It can be done right away.

3) 汉语无主语句和英语被动语态

汉语有一类句子不出现主语,在英语中可用被动语态表示:

昨天抓到了那个小偷。　　　　The thief was caught yesterday.

经过认真的讨论才得出结论。　　　　It was after a serious discussion that a conclusion was arrived at.

| 首先要保证质量。 | Quality must be guaranteed first. |

还有,汉语中有些措辞婉转的习语,或故意避免用主语,或用"有人"、"大家"之类泛指的主语,英译时,一般用以 it 作形式主语的被动结构,如:

据说……	It is said that...
希望……	It is hoped that...
据猜测……	It is supposed that...
必须承认……	It must be admitted that...
必须指出……	It must be pointed out that...
由此可以看出……	It will be seen that...
可以毫不夸张地说……	It may be said without fear of exaggeration that...
大家知道……	It is well known that...
有人会说……	It will be said that...
大家认为……	It is generally considered that...
有人相信……	It is believed that...
有人断言……	It is asserted that...

IMMEDIATE PRACTICE

Fill in the blanks with appropriate forms of the words given.

1. He begged _____ (forgive).

2. There was not a soul _____ (see) in the park.

3. This was a campaign _____ (wage) in the country.

4. They laughed, friendly and _____ (please).

5. The decision has to _____ (make).

6. Our house is getting _____ (paint).

7. In the rural areas of Shanghai agriculture is becoming more and more _____ (mechanize).

8. Will this meat _____ (keep) till tomorrow?

9. This poem _____ (read) well.

10. The cloth _____ (wash) well.

Translate the following sentences into English.

1. 据报导他们发现了一颗新星。

2. 她不喜欢把她当作小孩。

3. 他不希望在信里提及这个问题。

4. 有很多事要讨论。

5. 他把自己关在屋里以免被人打扰。

6. 获准在这里学习是难得的荣幸。

7. 他的梦想是获准进入一所好大学。

8. 她不能忍受这样的对待。

9. 正在盖的建筑物是一座音乐厅。

10. 去理一下发。

PART III TOWARD PRODUCTIVE LANGUAGE

READING ACTIVITIES

Read the following article very quickly and try to get the general meaning; do not worry if you come across some new words.

莫高窟被誉为 20 世纪最有价值的文化发现,坐落在河西走廊西端的敦煌,以精美的壁画和塑像闻名于世。但随着近年旅游业的发展,莫高窟的游客流量逐年迅速递增,珍贵而脆弱的壁画文物面临被毁坏的危险。为了保护世界文化遗产,国家明确提出了建立敦煌莫高窟数字化展示中心,这将有效地解决莫高窟保护与开发的矛盾。

Text B

History and Modern Technology
Unite in the Mogao Grottoes

Located on the eastern slope of Mingshashan,   southeast of Dunhuang County in Gansu Province,   the Mogao Grottoes is one of the three noted grottoes in China and also the largest,   best preserved and richest treasure house of Buddhist art in the world.

In AD 366, during the Eastern Jin Dynasty, a monk named Yue Zun chiseled the first cave here.
5 The endeavor continued through later dynasties,   including the Northern Wei (386—534), Western Wei (535—556), Northern Zhou (557—581), Sui (581—618), Tang (618—907), Five Dynasties (907—960), Song (960—1279), Western Xia (1038—1227) and Yuan (1279—1368), resulting in the fantastic group of caves that
10 can been seen. Today, 492 caves still stand, containing some 2,100 colored statues and 45,000 square meters of murals. These murals, if joined together, would cover a length of 30 kilometers. The caves vary in size. The

slope /sləʊp/ *n.* 倾斜,斜坡
grotto /ˈɡrɒtəʊ/ *n.* 岩穴,人造洞窟
noted /ˈnəʊtɪd/ *adj.* 著名的,知名的(for)
Buddhist /ˈbʊdɪst/ *n.* 佛教徒;*adj.* 佛教的
chisel /ˈtʃɪzəl/ *v.* 凿,刻
endeavor /ɪnˈdevə/ *n.* 努力,尽力
dynasty /ˈdɪnəstɪ/ *n.* 王朝,朝代
result in 导致,结果是
fantastic /fænˈtæstɪk/ *adj.* 奇异的,古怪的
statue /ˈstætjuː/ *n.* 雕像,铸像,塑像
mural /ˈmjʊərəl/ *n.* 壁画

131

smallest one just allows a head's space, while the largest one stretches from the foot to the top of the mountain, having a height of over 40 meters. The colored statues also differ in size, ranging from a few centimeters to 33 meters high, embodying the remarkable imagination of their makers.

Despite years of erosion, the murals are still brightly colored, with clear lines. Through pictures of different styles and schools drawn in different historical periods, they tell Buddhist stories and ways as well as life in the secular world. All these, plus a largest quantity of Buddhist sutras and relics kept in the caves have provided valuable material for a study of ancient China's politics, economy, and culture and arts, as well as its science and technology, military affairs, and religion, documenting national history as well as cultural exchanges between China and the world.

In 1987, UNESCO placed the Mogao Grottoes under the protection of the world cultural heritage list. In order to aid the grottoes conservation, The Dunhuang Academy has conducted numerous studies on the number and behavior of the visitors. After several years' preparation, they claim all those with an interest will be able to visit the world heritage Mogao Grottoes in northwest China by simply clicking a computer mouse.

Several years ago China decided to digitalize images of 170 of the finest Dunhuang grottoes. Of the images 147 are from the Mogao Grottoes and the rest of them from the Yulin Grottoes and Western Thousand Buddhas Caves.

Wang Xudong, deputy director of Dunhuang Academy, said high definition pictures of the grottoes, frescoes and colored sculptures would be taken. The three dimensional images would then be loaded onto an Internet database accessible to anyone.

Dunhuang Academy is the sole institute authorized to protect, research and manage the grotto treasures. Wang said the project was designed to protect and popularize the 1,600-year-old treasures and in

embody /ɪm'bɒdɪ/ *v.* 体现;包括,包含
erosion /ɪ'rəʊʒən/ *n.* 腐蚀,侵蚀,冲蚀
secular /'sekjʊlə/ *adj.* 尘世的;世俗的;非宗教的
sutra /'suːtrə/ *n.* 经文,经典
relic /'relɪk/ *n.* 遗物;圣物,圣骨
ancient /'eɪnʃənt/ *adj.* 古代的
military /'mɪlɪtərɪ/ *adj.* 军事的
document /'dɒkjʊmənt/ *v.* 用文件证明
as well as 也,又
heritage /'herɪtɪdʒ/ *n.* 遗产
fresco /'freskəʊ/ *n.* 壁画,用壁画法画的画
sculpture /'skʌlptʃə/ *n.* 雕刻,雕塑,雕像
dimensional /dɪ'menʃənəl/ *adj.* ……维的
authorize /'ɔːθəraɪz/ *v.* 授权,批准,认可
popularize /'pɒpjʊləraɪz/ *v.* 使普及;推广

particular the Mogao Grottoes.

Dunhuang became a very important market on the Silk Road in the Tang Dynasty (618—907) and is home
45 to more than 800 grottoes. The Mogao Grottoes were added to the World Heritage List in 1987.

schedule /'ʃedjuːl/ v. (时间的)预定,安排
initiate /ɪ'nɪʃieɪt/ v. 开始,创始;发动
decay /dɪ'keɪ/ n. 腐朽,衰退
inevitable /ɪn'evɪtəbəl/ adj. 不可避免的;
必然(发生)的
archaeologist /ˌɑːkɪ'ɒlədʒɪst/ n. 考古学家
loot /luːt/ v. 掠夺,抢劫

The number of people from China and abroad who visit the Dunhuang Grottoes is rising and will reach half a million in the near future, especially when a new train service goes into operation and additional flights are scheduled to the city of Dunhuang.

50 "The small grottoes are often packed with visitors and this poses a severe threat to the preservation of the frescoes and sculptures inside," said Wang. "That's why the 'Dunhuang Digital Program' was initiated."

Dunhuang Academy proposed the scheme in the early 1980s and subsequently reached a cooperation agreement with the US-based Andrew Mellon Foundation. The program now covers 20
55 grottoes.

"Decay of the artwork is almost inevitable but digital technology can provide a permanent library which can be used by both archaeologists and ordinary citizens," said Wang. "The 170 caves are like pearls on a crown and many of them are not open to visitors.

"In 2011 with a simple click of the mouse visitors will not only be able to appreciate the three
60 dimensional artworks in the grottoes but learn about their age, preservation measures and inspect details that cannot be seen clearly in the dim light on the spot," added Wang.

The Academy's database would include cultural relics looted by foreign archaeologists in the early twentieth century. "With the help of over 10 collectors and museums at home and abroad we'll survey all the relics available on Dunhuang culture and turn them into digital documents," said
65 Wang.

Zheng Binglin, director of the Dunhuang Studies Institute at Lanzhou University, felt the program would boost Dunhuang studies throughout the world. "It'll prompt more researchers to share their material and thus transform traditional research methods," Zheng said.

A *Choose the best answers for the following questions.*

1. Of all the images of the finest Dunhuang grottoes, which of the following place is not included?

   A. The Yulin Grottoes.   B. The Mogao Grottoes.

   C. The Singing Sands Mountain.   D. The Thousand Buddhas Caves.

2. What is the major reason that the Dunhuang Digital Program was proposed?

   A. It can meet the need of the people who can't afford the journey to Dunhuang.

   B. The big number of visitors threaten the preservation of the world heritage.

   C. The digitalized images can provide high definition pictures to the whole world easily.

   D. It's part of their task to the Dunhuang academy.

3. The phrase "high definition pictures" in Para 3 means _____.

   A. digitalized pictures   B. high quality pictures

   C. well-defined pictures   D. big and clear pictures

4. By 2012, you can appreciate _____ before your computer with a simple click of the mouse.

   A. the three dimensional artworks in the grottoes

   B. the preservation measures of the grottoes

   C. the age of the artworks

   D. all of the above

5. What is the passage mainly about?

   A. World cultural heritage unites with modern technology.

   B. An introduction to Dunhuang grottoes.

   C. Dunhuang grottoes in 2012.

   D. How Dunhuang grottoes became a cultural heritage.

B ***Answer the following questions.***

1. Where are the Mogao Grottoes located?

2. What leads to the fantastic group of caves that can be seen today?

3. What is the significance of these colored statues in the Mogao Grottoes?

4. According to the Dunhuang Academy, what measures can they take to deal with the decay of the artwork?

5. When were the Mogao Grottoes added to the World Heritage List?

Unit 8

PART I   PREPARATORY

WORDS IN CONTEXT

Read aloud the following sentences, paying attention to the meaning of the words in italics.

1. The issue of the death penalty is highly *controversial.*

2. There marriage seems to be extremely *problematic*.

3. In the end, it appeared a majority would not vote to *enshrine* a right to physician-assisted suicide.

4. For the school's deaf students, she *interpreted* the entire play in American Sign Language.

5. Julius Caesar *conquered* Gaul, which we know today as France.

6. Is anyone in domestic or foreign government stupid enough or *naive* enough to believe this?

7. However, seat belts also involve a degree of inconvenience, as *evidenced* by the unwillingness of many people to use them.

8. Money for the new health centre has come mostly from private *donors*.

9. The airliner was *hijacked* by a group of terrorists.

10. A smaller vehicle will *consume* less fuel.

WORDS LEARNED IN DISPLAY

Write the meaning of each of the following words in the corresponding blank.   You can write either in English or in Chinese.

controversial _____

problematic _____

enshrine _____

interpret _____

conquer _____

naive _____

evidence _____

donor _____

hijack _____

consume _____

EXPRESSIONS IN CONTEXT

Study the following expressions and see how they are used in sentences.

deal with 处理,对付,对待,打交道

◇ This problem is difficult to deal with.

embed in 使牢牢嵌入

◇ A piece of glass was embedded in her hand.

be preoccupied with 专心于,把思想集中于

◇ He's completely preoccupied with all the wedding preparations at the moment.

join hands with 与……携手合作;显示出与……的友谊

◇ The American soldiers joined hands with the British soldiers in the war against Germany.

conflict with 冲突

◇ In other ways the activities tend to conflict with regional policy and weaken its effects.

compare with (把……)与……相比

◇ How does your new house compare with your old one?

in conclusion 最后,综上所述

◇ In conclusion, she wished her colleagues every success in their work.

clamor for 大声地要求

◇ They clamored for the fair treatment.

EXPRESSIONS LEARNED IN DISPLAY

Complete each of the following sentences with the expressions you have just learned.

1. The audience cheered, _____ more.

2. The police_____ the suspect's fingerprints _____ those found at the crime scene.

3. _____, I want to thank all the people who have volunteered their time to our organization.

4. Do British immigration laws _____ any international laws?

5. He has learned how to _____ all kinds of complicated situations properly.

6. He _____ his name _____ the minds of millions of people.

7. He _____ far too _____ his own marital difficulties to give any thought to his friend's problems.

8. They _____ each other and danced round and round.

PART II LANGUAGE IN CONTEXT

GET YOURSELF INTERESTED

Read the following summary in Chinese and think what you are going to read in this text.

> 9·11 事件发生后,反对国际恐怖主义一跃成为美国对外政策日程的首位,国际社会也紧随其后,展开了对恐怖主义的"国际大围剿"。 随着阿富汗局势的发展,人们越来越认识到这的确是一场非对称性的战争。如果能够确定目标,反对恐怖主义的任务就像警察局办案一样干净利落。然而,最关键的问题是如何确定目标?美国曾开出一个恐怖主义国家的名单,包括阿富汗、伊拉克、利比亚、朝鲜等,这种确定方法是令人担忧的。如果这种确定方法成立的话,反对恐怖主义就会变成美国一个一个地"收拾"这些国家,它所引发的恶性循环对国际社会来说是一种灾难。

PREVIEW QUESTIONS

Work in pairs or groups and discuss the following questions.

1. Have you ever heard of September 11 attacks? What do you think of the attacks?

2. In your opinion, what is terrorism?

3. What do you think of Bush Administration's "War on Terror"?

War on Terrorism

We should not ignore the fact that the United States Constitution enshrined individual freedom of religious practice, which courts have since interpreted to mean that the government is a secular institution, an idea called "separation of church and state." This notion of separating religion from the state is one of the controversial aspects of exporting American culture.

5 This is embedded in the Bush administration's "War on Terror" which some have gone ahead to read as a war on Islam. This controversial American policy is what inspired Prof. Mamdani to write a book titled, *Good Muslim, Bad Muslim.*

America, which has thousands of military servicemen around the world, has of late been preoccupied with fighting terror in Afghanistan,

10 Iraq and it is getting ready to deal with the Iran problem soon. Actually some people are already speculating that the current crisis between Israel and Hezbollah is a precursor to America's war with Iran, that the US is supporting the Olmert

15 government to keep bombing Lebanon until Iran which is said to be the Godfather of Hezbollah gets angry enough to join the war. At this point it is argued that the US will join hands with Israel and fight the Iran government

20 because "they have weapons of mass destruction." At the end of the war as usual the US will be expected by many viewers to have conquered another oil producing country.

terrorism /'terərɪzəm/ *n.* 恐怖主义,恐怖手段

constitution /ˌkɒnstɪ'tjuːʃən/ *n.* 宪法,法规,章程

enshrine /ɪn'ʃraɪn/ *vt.* 放置或保存某物于……

interpret /ɪn'tɜːprɪt/ *vt.* 解释;口译

notion /'nəʊʃən/ *n.* 概念,观念,看法

controversial /ˌkɒntrə'vɜːʃəl/ *adj.* 有争议的,引起争议的

embed in 使牢牢嵌入

administration /əd,mɪnɪ'streɪʃən/ *n.* 管理;政府

policy /'pɒləsɪ/ *n.* 政策,方针

Muslim /'mʊzlɪm/ *n.* 穆斯林;伊斯兰教信徒

preoccupy /prɪ'ɒkjʊpaɪ/ *vt.* 占据(某人)思想,使对……全神贯注,使专心于

speculate /'spekjʊleɪt/ *vt. & vi.* 思索;猜测,推测

crisis /'kraɪsɪs/ *n.* 危机,危急关头

Hezbollah *n.* (黎巴嫩)真主党

precursor /prɪ'kɜːsə/ *n.* 先兆,前兆

bomb /'bɒm/ *v.* 轰炸,投弹

Many see the "War on Terror" as a veil for acquiring cheap oil to run the US economy.

25　Returning to the Israeli conflict with Hezbollah, one cannot fail to see an American tone in the whole conflict. Do you remember the first people to use the word "collateral damage"? This was what Americans first used to describe the death of innocent civilians and destruction of infrastructure by "precision" missiles during the Afghan war after the 9/11. This was an excuse used for having bombed the Chinese Embassy and a Red Cross facility during the war. Now

30　compare it with the death of thousand of Lebanese civilians and the destruction of hundreds of buildings. The death of UN officers and the recent Qana massacre can be accurately referred to as "collateral damage" by the Israeli government.

The apparent determination by the US to appoint itself "Mr. Fix it all" is a somewhat naive but optimistic belief among Americans that all problems can be fixed with enough commitment

35　and effort. This sometimes leads America into problematic situations such as Vietnam and Iraq. In some cases though, American-fix-it-all attitude has positively led to large outpouring of humanitarianism. This is clearly evidenced by the enormous aid that Americans, especially at the individual level, are sending to poor nations.

40　Americans like Bill Gates and CNN's Ted Turner are some of the world's biggest donors.

In conclusion, therefore, the global stage is at a period of American conquest in many different ways than you can imagine. Globalization seems to

45　be hijacked by the Americans. The world also seems to be clamoring for more of the Yankee lifestyle. However, simply dismissing—or demonizing—globalization as mere Americanization is misleading. Globalization has the ability to alter

50　much more than just the movies or food consumed by a society. And the results can be powerfully

conflict with 冲突
collateral damage 附带损害
civilian /sɪ'vɪljən/ n. 平民，百姓
infrastructure /'ɪnfrə,strʌktʃə/ n. 基础设施，基础结构
precision /prɪ'sɪʒən/ n. 精确度，准确(性)
missile /'mɪsaɪl/ n. 导弹，投射物
embassy /'embəsɪ/ n. 大使馆，大使馆全体成员
facility /fə'sɪlɪtɪ/ n. 设备，设施
massacre /'mæsəkə/ n. 大屠杀
apparent /ə'pærənt/ adj. 显然的，明白的，清晰可见的
naive /naɪ'iːv/ adj. 幼稚的；无经验的；单纯的
commitment /kə'mɪtmənt/ n. 承诺，许诺，保证
problematic /,prɒblə'mætɪk/ adj. 成问题的；有疑问的；疑难的；未定的
outpouring /'aʊtpɔːrɪŋ/ n. 倾泄，流出，流露
humanitarianism /hjuː'mænɪ'teərɪənɪzəm/ n. 人道主义，博爱主义
donor /'dəʊnə/ n. 捐赠者，赠与者
hijack /'haɪdʒæk/ vt. 劫持
clamour for 大声地要求
demonize /'diːmənaɪz/ vt. 使成为魔鬼，妖魔化

positive, devastatingly negative, or (more often) something in between.

> devastatingly /'devəsteɪtɪŋlɪ/ *adv.* 毁灭性地

COMPREHENSION CHECK

Understanding the General Ideas

Discuss the following questions in pairs or groups. The key words given in the brackets may help you in your discussion.

1. Why have some people gone ahead to read Bush administration's "War on Terror" as a war on Islam?

   (religion, government, export, interpret)

2. According to the passage, what do many viewers think of Bush administration's "War on Terror"?

   (conquer, oil, US economy)

3. By saying "Returning to the Israeli conflict with Hezbollah, one cannot fail to see an American tone in the whole conflict," what does the author mean?

   (Israeli, American, describe)

4. What impact does the US determination to appoint itself "Mr. Fix it all" have on itself and the world?

   (problematic, negative, positive, humanitarianism)

5. What is the author's opinion of "globalization" and "Americanization"?

   (the same, different, movies, food)

Understanding the Specifics

Read the following sentences and tell if they are true or false according to the text. In the brackets leading each statement, put "T" for true or "F" for false.

1. (　　) The US government prohibits its citizens from exporting American culture.

2. (　　) The US is supporting the Olmert government to keep bombing Lebanon because the Godfather of Hezbollah gets angry.

3. (　　) There is an American tone in the Israeli conflict with Hezbollah.

4. (　　) After 9/11, the US waged a war against Afghanistan.

5. (　　) Some American people are providing humanitarian aid to people in poor nations.

6. (　　) The Yankee lifestyle is a global lifestyle.

7. (　　) The author is cautious in presenting his opinion about the effects of globalization.

8. (　　) The author is not in favor of Bush administration's "War on Terror."

STUDY AND PRACTICE

Vocabulary

Fill in the blanks with the words below. Change the form where necessary.

controversial	interpret	conquer	naive
hijack	consume	inspire	precursor
commitment	problematic		

1. Whether any medicine can ever be found to cure cancer is ＿＿＿＿＿＿ .

2. We can hardly reach an absolute agreement on such a ＿＿＿＿＿＿ issue.

3. You _____ me by playing the piano so beautifully.

4. I _____ my dislike for mathematics.

5. Don't be so _____ as to be taken in by their lies.

6. The _____ of the modern car was a horseless carriage with a petrol engine.

7. The plane _____ soon after it took off.

8. He _____ a difficult passage in a book.

9. Arguing about details _____ many hours of the committee's valuable time.

10. He made a _____ to pay the rent on time.

Expressions

Rewrite the following sentences with the help of the phrases and expressions provided. The italicized part in each sentence may serve as the hint for your task. The first sentence is done for you.

in the name of	**embed in**	**clamor for**	**join hands with**
be preoccupied with	**conflict with**	**in conclusion**	**compare with**

1. When Tom *is absorbed in* his hobby he has no idea of what is going on around him.

   When Tom *is preoccupied with* his hobby he has no idea of what is going on around him.

2. They ought to *work together with* the workers and nip it in the mud.

   _____

3. The prime minister spoke *by the right of* the king.

   _____

4. The policeman's story *disagrees with* that of the accused.

   _____

5. The idea is *deeply fixed* in my mind.

6. *Finally*, I should like to say how much I have enjoyed myself.

7. This was leaked to the media, who began to *demand* stricter control.

8. *In comparison to* other recent video games, this one isn't very exciting.

Translation

A From Chinese to English

1. 她克服了恐惧,捡起了这个大蜘蛛。

2. 我把他的沉默理解为拒绝。

3. 他告诉她自己是王室的亲密朋友,她竟天真地相信他了。

4. 没多大一会儿饥饿的孩子们就吃掉了一块面包。

5. 我比较了印本和原件,但差别不是很大。

6. 下周来看我吧,那时我就不会像现在这样要把全部精力都投入到工作中了。

7. 我很累,因为我承担了很多的事情。

8. 我们不了解所有的情况,妄加推测是没有意义的。

B From English to Chinese

1. We should not ignore the fact that the United States Constitution enshrined individual freedom of religious practice, which courts have since interpreted to mean that the

government is a secular institution, an idea called "separation of church and state."

2. America, which has thousands of military servicemen around the world, has of late been preoccupied with fighting terror in Afghanistan, Iraq and it is getting ready to deal with the Iran problem soon.

3. Returning to the Israeli conflict with Hezbollah, one cannot fail to see an American tone in the whole conflict.

4. The apparent determination by the US to appoint itself "Mr. Fix it all" is a somewhat naive but optimistic belief among Americans that all problems can be fixed with enough commitment and effort.

5. Globalization has the ability to alter much more than just the movies or food consumed by a society. And the results can be powerfully positive, devastatingly negative, or (more often) something in between.

GRAMMAR

Subjunctive Mood (虚拟语气)

表示一种假想的情况或主观愿望时,动词需用一种特殊形式,称为虚拟语气。

1. 虚拟语气在条件句中的用法

表示纯然假想的条件句,称为虚拟条件句,在这类条件句中谓语动词需要用虚拟语气。

If I had enough money, I would buy a computer.

If you had arrived a little earlier, you would have seen her.

1) 表示现在和将来情况的虚拟条件句

(1) 条件从句中的谓语用过去时形式,主句谓语为 would(might 或 could)+ 动词原形。这类句子表示与事实相反的情况或实现可能性不大的情况:

If you left your bicycle outside, someone would steal it.

If I were you I'd plant some trees round the house.

If you tried again you might succeed.

If I knew her number I could ring her up.

在 if I were you 这样的句子中，were 不能改成 was，但在口语中第三人称单数后可以用 was。

(2) 在条件从句中有时还可以用"were to+ 不定式"或"should+ 不定式"这两种形式：

If he were to resign, who would take his place?

If you should have any difficulty in getting the medicine, (you could) ring this number.

(3) 在包括 were 或 should 的条件从句中，if 有时可省略，这时语序要改为倒装：

Were I Tom I would refuse.

Should you require anything just give me a call.

(4) 从句有时可用 if it were not for 这种句型，表示"若不是"：

If it weren't for your help, we would be in serious trouble.

Were it not for their loan, our life would be very difficult.

2）表示过去情况的虚拟条件句

(1) 条件从句中的谓语用过去完成时的形式，主句谓语通常用 would(could, might) have+ -ed 分词表示。这类从句表示与过去事实相反的情况：

If I had known that you were coming, I would have met you at the airport.

No doubt I could have earned something if I had really meant to.

If we had found him earlier we might have saved his life.

(2) 从句中也可用 had not been for 来构成谓语，表示"要不是"：

If it hadn't been for your timely help, we would have got into serious trouble.

If it hadn't been for Margaret, I might not have understood.

(3) if 有时可以省略，但后面部分需改为倒装语序：

Had she been asked, she would have done it.

Had I not seen it with my own eyes, I would not have believed it.

3) 一些特殊的虚拟条件句

（1）错综时间条件句

有些条件句主句谓语和从句谓语表示的动作在时间上并不一致，这类句子称为错综时间条件句(Conditional Sentences of Mixed Time)，如：

If he had received six more votes, he would be our chairman now.

If he had been trying hard, his parents wouldn't be so worried.

（2）含蓄条件句

有些句子里虽没有条件从句，但表达的却含有条件句的意思，这种句子称为含蓄条件句(Sentences of Implied Condition)，在这种句子中有时也需用虚拟语气：

I might see her personally, it would be better.

I would have written before but I have been ill.

But for my money that woman would have persecuted him.

Anybody else would have believed you.

2. 虚拟语气在某些从句中的运用

1）虚拟语气在宾语从句中的运用

（1）在 wish 后的宾语从句中，表示与事实相反的情况。用过去式表示现在的情况，动词 be 多用 were 形式；用相当于过去完成时的形式，表示过去的情况(常有遗憾的语气)：

I wish I knew what was going to happen.

I wish I were young again.

My father wishes (that) he had gone to university.

（2）would rather (sooner) 后的宾语从句，谓语用过去时的形式，表示现在或将来的情况；谓语用过去完成时的形式，表示过去的情况：

I'd rather you told me the truth.

I'd sooner you didn't ask me that question.

I'd rather you hadn't told me about it.

（3）在 suggest, order, demand, propose, command, request, desire, insist 等动词后

的宾语从句中，谓语动词一般要求用动词原形或用 should + 动词原形。

He suggested that a petition (should) be drawn up.

She demanded that I pay her immediately.

It was proposed that this matter be discussed at the next meeting.

2）虚拟语气在主语、表语等名词从句中的运用

（1）虚拟语气在主语从句中的使用：

It is important that he work hard.

It is essential that this mission not fail.

（2）用在表语从句的虚拟语气：

Our decision is that the school remain closed.

My suggestion is that we take the 6:00 train.

（3）用在同位语从句中的虚拟语气：

He made the suggestion that they carry on their conversation in Japanese.

There have been demands that the prime minister should resign.

3）虚拟语气在状语从句中的运用

（1）在 as if, as though 引导的方式状语从句中，表示现在情况时用过去虚拟语气，

表示过去情况时用过去完成时形式：

I have loved you as if you were my son.

He talks as though he knew where she was.

He talks about Rome as though he had been there himself.

Fancy you sitting there as if nothing had happened.

（2）有些目的状语从句也可用虚拟语气，谓语用动词原形，或用 should, would, could,

might+动词原形构成：

They removed the prisoner in order that he would not disturb the proceedings

any further.

The President must reject the proposal, lest it cause strife and violence.

He left early in order that the children would not be alone in the house.

I lent him $50 so that he might go for a holiday.

149

3. 虚拟语气的一些其他用法

1）在祝愿语中

God be praised!

God save all living beings!

May you enjoy many years of health and happiness.

May God bless you!

2）在 It's (high) time 后的从句中

It's time we went.

It's time we were leaving.

It's high time that you made up your mind.

IMMEDIATE PRACTICE

Fill in the blanks with the right forms of the verbs given in the brackets.

1. If you _____ (arrive) ten minutes earlier, you could have seen them off.

2. It's time that we _____ (go) to the railway station.

3. If they _____ (not help) us, our experiment would have failed.

4. You're five minutes late. I suggest that you _____ (come) earlier tomorrow.

5. Mother often tells us that it is necessary that we _____ (drink) a glass of water after

   we get up.

6. She insisted that she _____ (send) to work in the faraway small town.

7. _____ I not _____ (forget) his telephone number, I would have rung him.

8. He is busy now. If he _____ (be) free, he _____ (go) with you.

9. The manager was in his office then. If he _____ (be) here, everything _____

   (settle) in a minute.

10. Noisy as it was, he went on reading as if nothing _____ (happen).

Translate the following sentences into English.

1. 要是他在这儿，一切都没问题了。

2. 要是多穿点衣服你就不会着凉了。

3. 没有音乐，世界会很沉闷。

4. 我宁愿他们明天来。

5. 我提议定出一个交计划的期限。

6. 有必要马上派他到那里去。

7. 命令是我们仍留在原处。

8. 现在的确是结束这种做法的时候了。

9. 但愿你没有告诉我这一切。

10. 立即执行这项计划是很必要的。

READING ACTIVITIES

Read the following very quickly and try to get the general meaning; do not worry if you come across some new words.

> 你了解西方音乐吗？你了解西洋乐器吗？中世纪、文艺复兴时期、巴洛克时代、浪漫主义时代的器乐和乐器各有什么特点呢？本文将为你展开一幅西洋乐器的历史画卷。

Text B

The History of Instruments

Musical instruments are known to have existed in Europe over 25,000 years. The earliest examples were simple rhythm instruments used to emphasize man's own rhythm instruments of clapping hands and stamping feet. Many wind instruments, too, have a very long history. Bone, stone, wood, clay, and later metal were all used for making ancient instruments, which were
5 generally employed in signaling and ritual. The development of higher civilizations in the Middle East and Europe led to the evolution of more sophisticated instruments used for entertainment purposes. Contemporary literary and visual sources, together with surviving examples, prove the existence of a wide variety of instruments, and it is known that
10 the ancient Greeks and Romans in particular regarded their makers and performers with the highest esteem.

The Indian civilizations of Central and South America developed a rich musical culture of their own in the centuries before the arrival of the first
15 Europeans. Flutes, including whistles and panpipes,

musical instrument	乐器
rhythm /'rɪðəm/ n.	节奏，韵律
stamp /stæmp/ vt. & vi.	跺脚，顿足
clay /kleɪ/ n.	黏土，泥土
signaling /'sɪgnəlɪŋ/ n.	打信号，发信号
civilization /ˌsɪvəlaɪ'zeɪʃən/ n.	文明，文化
sophisticated /sə'fɪstɪkeɪtɪd/ adj.	精密的，复杂的
entertainment /ˌentə'teɪnmənt/ n.	娱乐，文娱节目
literary /'lɪtərəri/ adj.	文学(上)的
flute /fluːt/ n.	长笛，风管
whistle /'hwɪsəl/ n.	哨子；汽笛
panpipe /'pænpaɪp/ n.	排箫

were most important and a great variety of examples survive in museums. Rattles, scrapers, and drums were also significant, but interestingly there is no evidence of any stringed instruments at all.

Evidence from manuscripts, paintings, and church windows has been pieced together to provide an impression of the musical life of Medieval Europe. Few instruments survive from this
20 period, and sources suggest that the musical culture was less rich than that of the ancient civilizations of Greece and Rome. Certainly there was no clear distinction between folk and art music. Instruments were used mainly for the accompaniment of the voice, and drone instruments such as the hurdy-gurdy and bagpipes were favorites with medieval minstrels and troubadours. Very important in this period were Middle Eastern influence on the instruments of Western Europe. The
25 Arab Conquest of Spain and the return of Crusaders from the Middle East resulted in the introduction of previously unknown instruments and in modifications to those already in use.

In contrast with the Middle Ages, the renaissance was a period of intense musical activity in Europe. The most significant of the many musical developments in the years 1450 to 1650
30 was the rise in the importance of instrumental music. Beginning with the replacement of one or more of the melodic lines in a vocal piece, composers went on to write truly independent parts for instruments. A wealth of music was
35 specially written for consorts (small groups of instruments) such as recorders and viols and also for keyboards such as the harpsichord and organ. The rise of opera around 1600 in Italy was an important influence on the development of
40 instrumental music. Opera orchestras were assembled to accompany the singers, and composers first began to exploit the specific tone colors of individual instruments.

stringed /strɪŋd/ *adj.* 有弦(乐器)的
manuscript /'mænjəskrɪpt/ *n.* 手稿,原稿,底稿
medieval /ˌmedɪ'iːvəl/ *adj.* 中古的,中世纪的
distinction /dɪ'stɪŋkʃən/ *n.* 区别,明显差别;特征
accompaniment /ə'kʌmpənɪmənt/ *n.* 伴随物;伴奏
drone /drəʊn/ *n.* 持续的低音或和音
hurdy-gurdy /'hɜːdi'gɜːdi/ *n.* 一种乐器,手风琴之类
bagpipes /'bægpaɪps/ *n.* 风笛
minstrel /'mɪnstrəl/ *n.* 吟游诗人(或歌手)
troubadour /'truːbədʊə/ *n.* 行吟诗人,民谣歌手
crusader /kruː'seɪdə/ *n.* 十字军战士,改革者
modification /ˌmɒdɪfɪ'keɪʃən/ *n.* 更改
renaissance /rɪ'neɪsəns/ *n.* 文艺复兴,文艺复兴时期
replacement /rɪ'pleɪsmənt/ *n.* 代替,替换,更换
melodic /mɪ'lɒdɪk/ *adj.* 有旋律的,调子美妙的
consort /'kɒnsɔːt/ *n.* (演奏古典音乐的)一组乐师,一组古典乐器
recorder /rɪ'kɔːdə/ *n.* 雷高德(装有舌簧的八孔直笛)
viol /'vaɪəl/ *n.* 中世纪的六弦提琴
harpsichord /'hɑːpsɪkɔːd/ *n.* 羽管键琴,拨弦古钢琴
organ /'ɔːgən/ *vt.* 风琴
opera /'ɒpərə/ *n.* 歌剧,歌剧艺术,歌剧业
orchestra /'ɔːkɪstrə/ *n.* 管弦乐队
exploit /ɪk'splɔɪt/ *vt.* 开发;利用
tone color 音色

153

The baroque period, after 1650, saw the regular use of an ensemble which became the nucleus of the modern orchestra. It included the modern string group, flutes or recorders, oboes, bassoons, trumpets, and horns. Also characteristic was the continuo of keyboard and cello or bassoon provided to give a firm bass line and strengthen the harmonies. With the transition to the classical period around 1750, the continuo was abandoned and the orchestra enlarged with the addition of clarinets and occasionally trombones. Another important classical development was the enthusiastic adoption by most composers of the newly developed pianoforte.

The outstanding features of the romantic period, after 1830 were the rise of the virtuoso and the increasing influence of art and literature on music. The extraordinary technical gifts of such virtuoso performers as Paganini and Liszt encouraged composers to write more demanding parts both for soloists and the orchestral group as a whole. Interest in art and literature led composers to write descriptive pieces in the form of symphonic poems and concert overtures, which were freer both in content and in construction than the traditional symphony or concerto. Experiments in the field of instrument making gave rise to significant improvements to such instruments as the flute, trumpet, and piano. Several new instruments were also developed in the period, but only a few, like the tuba and saxophone, have survived to the 20th century.

Instrumental music of the 20th century may be divided into two broad groups. The first includes pieces for traditional resources in conventional forms such as the symphony, concerto, and sonata. The other comprises avant garde or "modern" music in which tapes and electronically produced sounds are used to supplement traditional instruments. Two new

baroque /bəˈrɒk/ *adj.* 巴罗克风格的,巴罗克风格流行时期的

ensemble /ɒŋˈsɒŋbəl/ *n.* 〈音〉合奏,合唱;合奏(或合唱)组

oboe /ˈəʊbəʊ/ *n.* 双簧管

bassoon /bəˈsuːn/ *n.* (一种吹奏乐器)巴松管,低音管

trumpet /ˈtrʌmpɪt/ *n.* 喇叭,小号

horn /hɔːn/ *n.* 铜管乐器,法国号

continuo /kənˈtɪnjʊəʊ/ *n.* 数字低音,数字低音部分

cello /ˈtʃeləʊ/ *n.* 大提琴

transition /trænˈzɪʃən/ *n.* 过渡;转变;变迁

clarinet /ˌklærɪˈnet/ *n.* 单簧管,竖笛

trombone /trɒmˈbəʊn/ *n.* 长号,伸缩长号

enthusiastic /ɪnˌθjuːzɪˈæstɪk/ *adj.* 满腔热情的,热心的;极感兴趣的

pianoforte /pɪˌænəʊˈfɔːti/ *n.* 钢琴(piano 的旧称)

virtuoso /ˌvɜːtjʊˈəʊzəʊ/ *n.* 艺术名家,乐器演奏大师

demanding /dɪˈmɑːdɪŋ/ *adj.* 要求高的,需要技能的,费力的

soloist /ˈsəʊləʊɪst/ *n.* 独奏(或独唱)演员

symphonic poem *n.* 交响诗

overture /ˈəʊvətjʊə/ *n.* (歌剧、芭蕾舞、音乐剧等的)序曲,前奏曲

concerto /kənˈtʃeətəʊ/ *n.* 协奏曲

tuba /ˈtjuːbə/ *n.* (乐器)大号

saxophone /ˈsæksəfəʊn/ *n.* 〈音〉萨克斯管

sonata /səˈnɑːtə/ *n.* 奏鸣曲

supplement /ˈsʌplɪment/ *vt.* 增补

types of instruments have made an impact on modem music and helped to bridge the gap between "popular" and "serious" musical styles. The first group — electro-mechanical—includes instruments such as the electric guitar in which the sound is produced mechanically but amplified or modified by electrical means. The second group comprises radio-electric instruments such as the electric organ and synthesizer in which the sound itself is produced electronically.

> electromechanical /ɪˌlektrəʊmɪˈkænɪkəl/ *adj.*
> 电动机械的,机电的,电机的
> electric guitar 电吉他
> amplify /ˈæmplɪfaɪ/ *vt.* 放大,扩大
> synthesizer /ˈsɪnθɪsaɪzə/ *n.* 合成器

75

READING COMPREHENSION

A **Choose the best answers for the following questions.**

1. The author develops his topic in a _____ order.

   A. chronological   B. spatial   C. relational   D. causal

2. The author mentions the Arab Conquest of Spain and the return of Crusaders from the Middle East to illustrate that _____.

   A. the musical culture of Mediaeval Europe was less rich than that of the Middle East

   B. the instruments of Western Europe were greatly influenced by the Middle East

   C. the instruments of Western Europe were brought to the Middle East at the time

   D. These are very important historic events in the Mediaeval Europe

3. Truly independent parts were written for instruments in _____ .

   A. the Middle Ages   B. the Renaissance

   C. the Baroque Period   D. the Classical Period

4. The phrase "give rise to" in the 6th paragraph most probably means_____.

   A. arise   B. give up

   C. lead to   D. increase

5. The author is _____ in presenting the information about the history of instruments.

    A. partial   B. radical   C. subjective   D. objective

B Answer the following questions.

1. How many musical instruments are mentioned in the text? What are they?

2. How many periods of development does the author mention as to the musical instruments in Europe?

3. What are the characteristics of each period?

4. Some people think that the renaissance is a crucial period in the development of instrumental mucic. Do you agree? Why or why not?

5. In what way(s) does modern technology contribute to the development of instrumental music and musical instruments?

Vocabulary

A

antiapartheid	/ˈæntɪəˈpɑːtheɪt/	adj.	反种族隔离的	Unit 3 – A
apart from			除了	Unit 2 – A
apparent	/əˈpærənt/	adj.	显然的,明白的,	
			清晰可见的	Unit 8 – A
appeal	/əˈpiːl/	n.	感染力,吸引力;呼吁,恳求	Unit 1 – B
appreciate	/əˈpriːʃieɪt/	vt.	欣赏	Unit 2 – A
archaeologist	/ˌɑːkɪˈɒlədʒɪst/	n.	考古学家	Unit 7 – B
argumentative	/ˌɑːgjʊˈmentətɪv/	adj.	好辩的,争论的	Unit 3 – B
aristocracy	/ˌærɪˈstɒkrəsɪ/	n.	贵族,贵族政权	Unit 7 – A
Aristotle	/ˈærɪstɒtl/	n.	亚里士多德(古希腊大	
			哲学家,科学家)	Unit 5 – B
arrogant	/ˈærəgənt/	adj.	傲慢的,自大的	Unit 3 – A
art fairs			艺术展览会	Unit 2 – A
artificial	/ˌɑːtɪˈfɪʃəl/	adj.	人造的,人工的;假的	Unit 6 – B
as well as			也,又	Unit 7 – B
aspiring	/əsˈpaɪərɪŋ/	adj.	有追求的	Unit 3 – A
assemble	/əˈsembəl/	vt.& vi.	集合,收集,装配,组合	Unit 5 – A
assimilation	/əsɪmɪˈleɪʃən/	n.	(被)吸收或同化的过程	Unit 6 – B
at large			一般来说;普遍;充分地,	
			全面地	Unit 7 – A
at the instant			一……就……	Unit 1 – A
at the moment			此刻,目前	Unit 1 – A
atmosphere	/ˈætməsfɪə/	n.	气氛,环境	Unit 2 – B
authentic	/ɔːˈθentɪk/	adj.	真的,真正的	Unit 6 – B
authority	/ɔːˈθɒrɪtɪ/	n.	权力,当权的地位;当权者;	
			[复数]当局,官方	Unit 7 – A
authorize	/ˈɔːθəraɪz/	v.	授权,批准,认可	Unit 7 – B
automatic	/ɔːtəˈmætɪk/	adj.	自动的;不假思索的;	
			无意识的	Unit 4 – B

avante garde	/ˌævɒŋˈgɑːd/		(法)前卫	Unit 7 – A

B

baggy	/ˈbægɪ/	adj.	宽松下垂的	Unit 1 – B
bagpipes	/ˈbægpaɪps/	n.	风笛	Unit 8 – B
balanced diet		n.	均衡的饮食	Unit 4 – A
baroque	/bəˈrɒk/	adj.	巴罗克风格的,巴罗克风格流行时期的	Unit 8 – B
basement	/ˈbeɪsmənt/	n.	地下室	Unit 4 – A
bassoon	/bəˈsuːn/	n.	(一种吹奏乐器)巴松管,低音管	Unit 8 – B
be likely to			有可能	Unit 3 – B
be limited in			限制于	Unit 7 – A
be obliged to			不得不	Unit 7 – A
be renowned for			以……著称	Unit 2 – A
bedwetting		n.	尿床,遗尿	Unit 4 – B
beloved	/bɪˈlʌvɪd/	adj.	敬爱的	Unit 7 – A
benevolent	/bɪˈnevələnt/	adj.	慈善的	Unit 7 – A
be / get used to			习惯于……的	Unit 3 – B
blood vessel			血管	Unit 4 – B
board	/bɔːd/	n.	板,牌子	Unit 1 – A
boldness	/ˈbəʊldnɪs/	n.	大胆,冒失	Unit 3 – A
bomb	/ˈbɒm/	v.	轰炸,投弹	Unit 8 – A
bottle up			克制,抑制,约束	Unit 4 – A
break up			结束;破裂	Unit 5 – A
breed	/briːd/	n.	种,种类,品种	Unit 5 – A
Bretton Woods Institutions			布雷顿森林机构,指 IMF 和世界银行	Unit 6 – B
broad jump			跳远	Unit 1 – A
broaden	/ˈbrɔːdn/	vt.	拓宽	Unit 2 – A

bubble	/'bʌbəl/	vt. & vi.	起泡,使冒气泡	
		n.	水泡,气泡;泡影	Unit 5 – B
buckle	/'bʌkəl/	n.	搭扣,扣环	Unit 6 – A
Buddhist	/'budɪst/	n.	佛教徒	
		adj.	佛教的	Unit 7 – B
bungy-jump		n.	蹦极	Unit 1 – B

C

cabinet	/'kæbɪnɪt/	n.	小屋;橱柜	Unit 7 – A
carat	/'kærət/	n.	开(黄金纯度单位)	Unit 1 – A
care about			在乎,在意	Unit 3 – A
casino	/kə'siːnəu/	n.	赌场,娱乐场	Unit 6 – A
celebrity	/sɪ'lebrɪti/	n.	(尤指娱乐界的) 名人,名流	Unit 3 – A
cello	/'tʃeləu/	n.	大提琴	Unit 8 – B
cemetery	/'semɪtrɪ/	n.	墓地,公墓	Unit 7 – A
cereal	/'sɪərɪəl/	n.	谷类植物;谷物	Unit 4 – A
challenge	/'tʃælɪndʒ/	n.	挑战	Unit 4 – A
character	/'kærɪktə/	n.	特征,性质,性格	Unit 7 – A
childishly	/'tʃaɪldɪʃli/	adv.	天真地;幼稚地	Unit 1 – A
chirp	/tʃɜːp/	vi.	鸟叫;虫鸣	Unit 5 – B
chisel	/'tʃɪzəl/	v.	凿,刻	Unit 7 – B
chore	/'tʃɔː/	n.	零工,杂务;令人疲劳不愉快的工作	Unit 3 – B
chronic	/'krɒnɪk/	adj.	长期患病的;慢性的	Unit 5 – B
civilian	/sɪ'vɪljən/	n.	平民,百姓	Unit 8 – A
civilization	/ˌsɪvəlaɪ'zeɪʃən/	n.	文明,文化	Unit 8 – B
clamour for			大声地要求	Unit 8 – A
clarinet	/ˌklærɪ'net/	n.	单簧管,竖笛	Unit 8 – B

clash with			发生冲突;与……不协调	Unit 3 – B
clay	/kleɪ/	n.	黏土,泥土	Unit 8 – B
cleric	/'klerɪk/	n.	牧师,教士,神职人员	Unit 3 – A
collateral damage			附带损害	Unit 8 – A
colonialism	/kə'ləʊnɪəlɪzəm/	n.	殖民主义,殖民政策	Unit 6 – B
combination	/ˌkɒmbɪ'neɪʃən/	n.	结合,组合	Unit 2 – B
come into being			开始存在	Unit 2 – A
commentary	/'kɒməntərɪ/	n.	实况报道;评论	Unit 6 – B
commitment	/kə'mɪtmənt/	n.	承诺,许诺,保证	Unit 8 – A
common good			公益	Unit 3 – A
communication	/kəˌmjuːnɪ'keɪʃən/	n.	交流	Unit 2 – A
concentrate on			将……集中于……	Unit 2 – A
concerto	/kən'tʃeətəʊ/	n.	协奏曲	Unit 8 – B
concurrently	/kən'kʌrəntlɪ/	adv.	同时存在(发生、完成)	Unit 6 – B
conduit	/'kɑːndʊɪt/	n.	管道,渠道	Unit 6 – A
conflict with			冲突	Unit 8 – A
confusing	/kən'fjuːzɪŋ/	adj.	令人困惑的	Unit 3 – B
connotation	/kɒnə'teɪʃən/	n.	内涵意义,隐含意义	Unit 6 – B
conquer	/'kɒŋkə/	vt.	攻克;征服;克服	Unit 3 – A
consequence	/'kɒnsɪkwəns/	n.	结果,后果	Unit 3 – A
consequently	/'kɒnsɪkwəntlɪ/	adv.	所以,因此	Unit 6 – B
conservationist	/ˌkɒnsə'veɪʃənɪst/	n.	自然资源保护者, 生态环境保护者	Unit 3 – A
consort	/'kɒnsɔːt/	n.	(演奏古典音乐的)一组乐师, 一组古典乐器	Unit 8 – B
constant	/'kɒnstənt/	adj.	恒久不变的;不断的	Unit 5 – A
constitution	/ˌkɒnstɪ'tjuːʃən/	n.	宪法,法规,章程	Unit 8 – A
consume	/kən'sjuːm/	vt.	消耗,消费,耗尽	Unit 2 – B
contemporary	/kən'tempɒrərɪ/	adj.	当代的;同时代的	Unit 6 – B

contestant	/kən'testənt/	n.	竞争者；参赛者	Unit 1 – B
continental	/ˌkɒntɪ'nentəl/	adj.	大陆的，大陆性的，欧洲大陆的	Unit 6 – A
continuo	/kən'tɪnjuəu/	n.	数字低音，数字低音部分	Unit 8 – B
contribute to			捐献，贡献	Unit 7 – A
contribution	/ˌkɒntrɪ'bjuːʃən/	n.	捐助物；贡献	Unit 3 – A
controversial	/ˌkɒntrə'vɜːʃəl/	adj.	有争议的，引起争议的	Unit 8 – A
cope with			(成功地)应付；妥善地处理	Unit 4 – A
corporate	/'kɔːpərət/	aaj.	企业的，法人的	Unit 6 – B
counter	/'kauntə/	vt. & vi.	对抗；反驳	Unit 4 – A
counteract	/kauntər'ækt/	vt.	对抗；抵消	Unit 4 – B
cricket	/'krɪkɪt/	n.	蟋蟀；板球	Unit 5 – B
crisis	/'kraɪsɪs/	n.	危机，危急关头	Unit 8 – A
critical	/'krɪtɪkəl/	adj.	决定性的，关键性的；危急的；批评的，批判的	Unit 3 – A
crooner	/'kruːnə/	n.	低声唱歌的人或歌手	Unit 5 – A
crouch	/krautʃ/	vi.	屈膝，蹲伏	Unit 2 – B
crusader	/kruː'seɪdə/	n.	十字军战士，改革者	Unit 8 – B
cuisine	/kwɪ'ziːn/	n.	烹饪艺术，菜肴	Unit 6 – A

D

daredevil	/'deədevəl/	adj.	鲁莽大胆的	Unit 1 – B
date back to			回溯至	Unit 5 – A
deadline	/'dedlaɪn/	n.	最后期限	Unit 4 – B
decay	/dɪ'keɪ/	n.	腐朽，衰退	Unit 7 – B
dedicate oneself to			专心致力于	Unit 7 – A
defecation	/defə'keɪʃn/	n.	澄清，净化；通便	Unit 4 – B
deficiency	/dɪ'fɪʃənsi/	n.	缺乏，不足	Unit 4 – A
demanding	/dɪ'mɑːdɪŋ/	adj.	要求高的，需要技能的，费力的	Unit 8 – B

demonize	/'diːmənaɪz/	vt.	使成为魔鬼,妖魔化	Unit 8 – A
demonstrate	/'demənstreɪt/	vi.	显示,表露	Unit 6 – A
depend on			依赖,依靠	Unit 2 – B
dependent	/dɪ'pendənt/	adj.	依靠的,依赖的	Unit 2 – A
descendant	/dɪ'sendənt/	n.	后代,后裔	Unit 2 – B
deserted	/dɪ'zɜːtɪd/	adj.	荒芜的,人迹罕至的	Unit 4 – A
despise	/dɪ'spaɪz/	vt.	鄙视,看不起某人(某事)	Unit 6 – A
deteriorate	/dɪ'tɪərɪəreɪt/	vi.	恶化,变坏	Unit 4 – B
devastatingly	/'devəsteɪtɪŋlɪ/	adv.	毁灭性地	Unit 8 – A
dietitian	/ˌdaɪə'tɪʃən/	n.	饮食学家,营养学家,膳食学家	Unit 6 – A
digital	/'dɪdʒɪtl/	adj.	数字式的,数码的,数字显示的	Unit 6 – A
dilate	/daɪ'leɪt/	vt. & vi.	(使某物)扩大,膨胀,张大	Unit 4 – B
dimension	/daɪ'menʃən/	n.	维度,规模,程度	Unit 6 – B
dimensional	/dɪ'menʃənəl/	adj.	……维的	Unit 7 – B
dirt	/dɜːt/	n.	泥土;污垢	Unit 1 – A
disciple	/dɪ'saɪpəl/	n.	弟子,门徒	Unit 7 – A
discipline	/'dɪsɪplɪn/	v.	严格要求自己;约束自己	Unit 1 – A
disgustedly	/dɪs'gʌstɪdli/	adv.	厌恶地	Unit 1 – A
disparate	/'dɪspərət/	adj.	根本不同的,不能相比较的 Unit 6 – B
distinction	/dɪ'stɪŋkʃən/	n.	区别,明显差别;特征	Unit 8 – B
distinguished	/dɪ'stɪŋgwɪʃt/	adj.	卓越的;著名的;受人尊敬的	Unit 3 – A
distract	/dɪ'strækt/	vt.	使(人)分心;分散(注意力)	Unit 4 – A
doctrine	/'dɒktrɪn/	n.	教条,学说	Unit 7 – A
document	/'dɒkjʊmənt/	v.	用文件证明	Unit 7 – B
domestic	/də'mestɪk/	adj.	国内的;家庭的;家养的	Unit 2 – A
dominate	/'dɒmɪneɪt/	vt. & vi.	控制,统治;耸立于,俯临	Unit 5 – A
donor	/'dəʊnə/	n.	捐赠者,赠与者	Unit 8 – A
dream of			做梦(梦见)	Unit 3 – A
drone	/drəʊn/	n.	持续的低音或和音	Unit 8 – B

dual-track			双轨的	Unit 2 – A
due to			由于	Unit 2 – A
dynasty	/'dɪnəstɪ/	n.	王朝,朝代	Unit 7 – B
dyslexics	/dɪs'leksɪks/	n.	诵读困难者	
		adj.	诵读困难的	Unit 5 – B

E

eating joint			〈美俚〉小饭馆	Unit 6 – A
educationist	/ˌedjʊ'keɪʃənɪst/	n.	教育家	Unit 7 – A
electric guitar			电吉他	Unit 8 – B
electromechanical	/ɪˌlektrəʊmɪ'kænɪkəl/	adj.	电动机械的,机电的,电机的	Unit 8 – B
electronic media			电子宣传工具(指广播、电视)	Unit 6 – A
embassy	/'embəsɪ/	n.	大使馆,大使馆全体成员	Unit 8 – A
embed in			使牢牢嵌入	Unit 8 – A
embody	/ɪm'bɒdɪ/	v.	体现;包括,包含	Unit 7 – B
emerge	/ɪ'mɜːdʒ/	vi.	出现,显出	Unit 2 – A
emotional	/ɪ'məʊʃənəl/	adj.	感情上的;令人动情的	Unit 4 – A
empire	/'empaɪə/	n.	帝国	Unit 2 – A
endeavor	/ɪn'devə/	n.	努力,尽力	Unit 7 –
energetic	/ˌenə'dʒetɪk/	adj.	精力充沛的,充满活力的	Unit 2 – B
enormous	/ɪ'nɔːməs/	adj.	巨大的,极大的	Unit 4 – A
ensemble	/ɒn'sɒŋbəl/	n.	〈音〉合奏,合唱;合奏(或合唱)组	Unit 8 – B
enshrine	/ɪn'ʃraɪn/	vt.	放置或保存某物于……	Unit 8 – A
entertainment	/ˌentə'teɪnmənt/	n.	娱乐,文娱节目	Unit 8 – B
enthusiastic	/ɪnˌθjuːzɪ'æstɪk/	adj.	满腔热情的,热心的;	
			极感兴趣的	Unit 8 – B
equivalent	/ɪ'kwɪvələnt/	n.	同等物,等价物,相等物	Unit 6 – A
era	/'ɪərə/	n.	纪元;历史时期,时代	Unit 5 – A
erosion	/ɪ'rəʊʒən/	n.	腐蚀,侵蚀,冲蚀	Unit 7 – B

essential	/ɪˈsenʃəl/	adj.	必不可少的;非常重要的	Unit 1 – A
establish	/ɪsˈtæblɪʃ/	vt.	建立,成立	Unit 3 – B
esteem	/ɪˈstiːm/	n.	尊敬;好评	Unit 4 – B
eventful	/ɪˈventfəl/	adj.	充满大事的,重大的	Unit 7 – A
everlasting	/ˌevəˈlɑːstɪŋ/	adj.	永恒的,持久的	Unit 7 – A
exception	/ɪkˈsepʃən/	n.	例外	Unit 1 – A
excessive	/ɪkˈsesɪv/	adj.	过度的;过分的;极度的	Unit 4 – A
exertion	/ɪgˈzɜːʃən/	n.	用力,努力,费力	Unit 1 – B
expect	/ɪkˈspekt/	v.	预料,希望	Unit 1 – A
explode with			突然发作	Unit 4 – A
exploit	/ɪkˈsplɔɪt/	vt.	开发;利用	Unit 8 – B
external	/ɪkˈstɜːnl/	adj.	外面的,外部的	Unit 4 – A
extreme	/ɪkˈstriːm/	adj.	极度的,极端的;过激的	Unit 1 – B

F

facility	/fəˈsɪlɪtɪ/	n.	设备,设施	Unit 8 – A
fake	/feɪk/	adj.	假的,冒充的	Unit 1 – A
fantastic	/fænˈtæstɪk/	adj.	奇异的,古怪的	Unit 7 – B
fascinate	/ˈfæsɪneɪt/	vt.	使着迷,使极感兴趣	Unit 6 – B
financial	/faɪˈnænʃəl/	adj.	经济上的,财政的	Unit 2 – A
financial flow			资金流量	Unit 6 – B
flute	/fluːt/	n.	长笛,风管	Unit 8 – B
focus on			集中注意力于;使聚焦于	Unit 4 – A
format	/ˈfɔːmæt/	v.	安排,计划	Unit 6 – B
foul /faʊl/		v.	〈体〉(对……)犯规	
		n.	犯规	Unit 1 – A
franchise	/ˈfræntʃaɪz/	n.	特许经营,特许权,专营权	Unit 6 – A
fresco	/ˈfreskəʊ/	n.	壁画,用壁画法画的画	Unit 7 – B
frustrated	/ˈfrʌstreɪtɪd/	adj.	挫败的,失望的,泄气的	Unit 3 – B

frustration	/frʌˈstreɪʃən/	n.	挫败,挫折,受挫	Unit 4 – A
fulfill	/fʊlˈfɪl/	vt.	实现,履行	Unit 2 – A
fundamental	/ˌfʌndəˈmentl/	adj.	基本的;重要的;必要的	Unit 3 – A

G

gadget	/ˈɡædʒɪt/	n.	小机械,小器具	Unit 6 – A
gain from			从……获得	Unit 3 – A
gear	/ɡɪə/	n.	用具;设备;衣服	Unit 1 – B
generation	/ˌdʒenəˈreɪʃən/	n.	一代人,一代	Unit 3 – A
gigantic	/dʒaɪˈɡæntɪk/	adj.	巨大的,庞大的	Unit 6 – A
glare at			用(愤怒的)目光注视	Unit 1 – A
globalization	/ɡləʊbəlaɪˈzeɪʃən/	n.	全球化,全球性	Unit 6 – B
goodwill	/ˈɡʊdˈwɪl/	n.	善意,亲切,友好	Unit 3 – A
grip	/ɡrɪp/	n.	紧握;紧咬;阵痛	Unit 1 – A
grotto	/ˈɡrɒtəʊ/	n.	岩穴,人造洞窟	Unit 7 – B

H

hamper	/ˈhæmpə/	vt.	妨碍,束缚,限制	Unit 3 – A
harmony	/ˈhɑːmənɪ/	n.	和谐,协调	Unit 5 – A
harpsichord	/ˈhɑːpsɪkɔːd/	n.	羽管键琴,拨弦古钢琴	Unit 8 – B
have sth/sb in mind			心中考虑到某物 / 某人	Unit 1 – A
heartburn	/ˈhɑːtbɜːn/	n.	胃灼热,烧心	Unit 4 – B
heritage	/ˈherɪtɪdʒ/	n.	遗产	Unit 7 – B
Hezbollah		n.	(黎巴嫩)真主党	Unit 8 – A
hijack	/ˈhaɪdʒæk/	vt.	劫持	Unit 8 – A
hip-hop		n.	嘻哈	Unit 6 – A
horn	/hɔːn/	n.	铜管乐器,法国号	Unit 8 – B
humanitarianism	/hjuːˈmænɪˈteərɪənɪzəm/	n.	人道主义,博爱主义	Unit 8 – A

humiliate	/hjuˈmɪlieɪt/	vt.	使蒙羞,羞辱,使丢脸	Unit 3 – A
hurdy-gurdy	/ˈhɜːdiˈɡɜːdi/	n.	一种乐器,手风琴之类	Unit 8 – B
hype	/haɪp/	n.	天花乱坠的广告宣传	Unit 1 – B
hyperactive	/haɪpəˈræktɪv/	adj.	活动过度的,极度活跃的,	
			活动亢进的	Unit 4 – B

I

ideal	/aɪˈdɪəl/	n.	理想	Unit 7 – A
identifiable	/aɪˈdentɪfaɪəbəl/	adj.	可以确认的,可以识别的	Unit 5 – A
identify	/aɪˈdentɪfaɪ/	vt.	识别;确定	Unit 4 – A
identity	/aɪˈdentɪti/	n.	身份;个性;特性	Unit 3 – B
ideological	/ˌaɪdɪəˈlɒdʒɪkəl/	adj.	意识形态的	Unit 7 – A
imitate	/ˈɪmɪteɪt/	vt.	模仿	Unit 5 – B
imitation	/ˌɪmɪˈteɪʃn/	n.	模仿,仿效;仿制品,伪造物	Unit 6 – A
immigrant	/ˈɪmɪɡrənt/	n.	移民	Unit 6 – A
impart	/ɪmˈpɑːt/	v.	传授	Unit 7 – A
impending	/ɪmˈpendɪŋ/	adj.	即将发生的,迫在眉睫的	Unit 4 – B
imperialism	/ɪmˈpɪərɪəlɪzəm/	n.	帝国主义,帝国主义政策	Unit 6 – B
in a strict sense			严格说来	Unit 2 – A
in one's hands			由某人支配/控制/掌管	Unit 3 – B
in the wake of			尾随,紧跟,仿效	Unit 5 – A
inducing	/ɪnˈdjuːsɪŋ/	adj.	产生诱导作用的	Unit 4 – A
inelegant	/ɪnˈelɪɡənt/	adj.	不雅的,粗俗的	Unit 2 – A
inevitable	/ɪnˈevɪtəbəl/	adj.	不可避免的;必然(发生)的	Unit 7 – B
influence	/ˈɪnfluəns/	vt.	影响	Unit 2 – A
infrastructure	/ˈɪnfrəˌstrʌktʃə/	n.	基础设施,基础结构	Unit 8 – A
inhibition	/ˌɪnhɪˈbɪʃən/	n.	抑制	Unit 6 – B
initiate	/ɪˈnɪʃieɪt/	v.	开始,创始;发动	Unit 7 – B

insist	/ɪnˈsɪst/	v.	坚持，坚持认为	Unit 1 – A
insomnia	/ɪnˈsɒmnɪə/	n.	〈医〉失眠(症)	Unit 5 – B
instantaneous	/ˌɪnstənˈteɪnɪəs/	adj.	瞬间发生的，即刻的	Unit 4 – B
integration	/ˌɪntɪˈɡreɪʃən/	n.	结合，整合，一体化	Unit 6 – B
integrity	/ɪnˈteɡrɪtɪ/	n.	正直，诚实	Unit 7 – A
intellect	/ˈɪntəlekt/	n.	文人，知识分子	Unit 7 – A
interaction	/ˌɪntərˈækʃən/	n.	互动，相互作用	Unit 3 – B
International Monetary Fund		n.	国际货币基金会	Unit 6 – B
interpret	/ɪnˈtɜːprɪt/	vt.	解释；口译	Unit 8 – A
intersect	/ɪntəˈsekt/	vt. & vi.	(指线条、道路等)相交，交叉	Unit 5 – B
intractable	/ɪnˈtræktəbəl/	adj.	难对付的，难解决的	Unit 3 – A
investment	/ɪnˈvestmənt/	n.	投资	Unit 2 – A
iPod			音乐播放器	Unit 6 – A
irritable	/ˈɪrɪtəbəl/	adj.	易怒的，急躁的	Unit 4 – B

J

jazz	/dʒæz/	n.	爵士乐	Unit 6 – A
joyous	/ˈdʒɔɪəs/	adj.	快乐的，使人喜悦的	Unit 2 – B
junk food		n.	垃圾食品，无营养食品	Unit 6 – A

K

keep at bay			控制	Unit 5 – B
kick	/kɪk/	v.	踢	Unit 1 – A
knock out			使筋疲力尽；使竭尽全力；粗略地[匆匆地]创作[完成]	Unit 3 – A

L

lap	/læp/	n.	(坐着时)膝上腰下的大腿部分	Unit 4 – A

168

laptop	/'læptɒp/	n.	便携式电脑	Unit 6 – B
lead	/li:d/	n.	主角,主要演员	Unit 3 – B
leap	/li:p/	vi.	跳,跳跃	Unit 2 – B
let off steam			宣泄被压抑的感情;发牢骚;	
			散发多余的精力	Unit 4 – A
leverage	/'li:vərɪdʒ/	n.	力量,影响	Unit 6 – B
liberalization	/ˌlɪbərəlaɪzeɪʃən/	n.	自由主义化,使宽大	Unit 6 – B
literary	/'lɪtə rəri/	adj.	文学(上)的	Unit 8 – B
longstanding	/'lɒŋ'stændɪŋ/	adj.	持久的	Unit 3 – B
loot	/lu:t/	v.	掠夺,抢劫	Unit 7 – B

M

maintain	/meɪn'teɪn/	vt.	保持;继续	Unit 4 – A
make a mess (of)			(把……)弄糟[搞坏];	
			(把……)搞得一塌糊涂	Unit 3 – A
make demand on			提出要求,有求于	Unit 4 – A
make use of			利用,使用	Unit 7 – A
manifest	/'mænɪfest/	vt.	清楚表示;显露	Unit 4 – A
manufacture	/ˌmænjə'fæktʃə/	vt.	制造;捏造	Unit 5 – A
manuscript	/'mænjəskrɪpt/	n.	手稿,原稿,底稿	Unit 8 – B
mask	/mɑ:sk/	n.	口罩;面具;掩饰	Unit 3 – A
massacre	/'mæsəkə/	n.	大屠杀	Unit 8 – A
measure	/'meʒə/	n.	量度,测量	Unit 2 – A
medieval	/ˌmedɪ'i:vəl/	adj.	中古的,中世纪的	Unit 8 – B
meditation	/ˌmedɪ'teɪʃən/	n.	默想;沉思	Unit 4 – A
meditative	/'medɪtətɪv/	adj.	沉思的,冥想的	Unit 5 – B
melodic	/mɪ'lɒdɪk/	adj.	有旋律的,调子美妙的	Unit 8 – B
merger	/'mɜ:dʒə/	n.	(两个公司的)合并	Unit 5 – B

mess	/mes/	n.	杂乱,脏乱	Unit 3 – A
migraine	/ˈmiːɡreɪn/	n.	偏头痛	Unit 4 – B
military	/ˈmɪlɪtərɪ/	adj.	军事的	Unit 7 – B
mineral	/ˈmɪnərəl/	n.	矿物质;矿石	Unit 4 – A
minstrel	/ˈmɪnstrəl/	n.	吟游诗人(或歌手)	Unit 8 – B
missile	/ˈmɪsaɪl/	n.	导弹,投射物	Unit 8 – A
modification	/ˌmɒdɪfɪˈkeɪʃən/	n.	更改	Unit 8 – B
morality	/məˈrælɪtɪ/	n.	道德	Unit 7 – A
multinational	/mʌltɪˈnæʃənəl/	adj.	多国的	Unit 6 – B
mural	/ˈmjʊərəl/	n.	壁画	Unit 7 – A
muscle spasm			肌肉痉挛	Unit 4 – B
muscular	/ˈmʌskjʊlə/	adj.	(有关)肌(肉)的;强壮的	Unit 4 – A
musical instrument			乐器	Unit 8 – B
Muslim	/ˈmʊzlɪm/	n.	穆斯林;伊斯兰教信徒	Unit 8 – A

N

naive	/nɑːˈiːv/	adj.	幼稚的;无经验的;单纯的	Unit 8 – A
nationalistic	/ˌnæʃənəˈlɪstɪk/	adj.	民族(国家主义的)	Unit 1 – A
no matter			无论	Unit 3 – B
noradrenaline	/ˌnɔːrəˈdrenəlɪn/	n.	去甲肾上腺素	Unit 4 – B
noted	/ˈnəʊtɪd/	adj.	著名的,知名的(for)	Unit 7 – B
notion	/ˈnəʊʃən/	n.	概念,观念,看法	Unit 8 – A
numerous	/ˈnjuːmərəs/	adj.	很多的,许多的	Unit 6 – A
nutrient	/ˈnjuːtriənt/	n.	(食品或化学品)营养物,营养品	Unit 4 – A

O

oasis	/əʊˈeɪsɪs/	n.	绿洲	Unit 3 – A
obesity	/əʊˈbiːsɪti/	n.	肥胖,肥大	Unit 6 – A

objective	/əb'dʒektɪv/	n.	目的,目标	Unit 7 – A
oboe	/'əubəu/	n.	双簧管	Unit 8 – B
obsess	/əb'ses/	vt.	时刻困扰;缠住	Unit 5 – B
obsession	/əb'seʃən/	n.	困扰;无法摆脱的思想 (或情感)	Unit 4 – B
official	/ə'fɪʃəl/	adj.	官方的	Unit 2 – A
opera	/'ɒpərə/	n.	歌剧,歌剧艺术,歌剧业	Unit 8 – B
orchestra	/'ɔːkɪstrə/	n.	管弦乐队	Unit 5 – A
orchestra	/'ɔːkɪstrə/	n.	管弦乐队	Unit 8 – B
organ	/'ɔːgən/	vt.	风琴	Unit 8 – B
organization	/ˌɔːgənaɪ'zeɪʃən/	n.	组织,机构,团体	Unit 2 – B
outpouring	/'autpɔːrɪŋ/	n.	倾泄,流出,流露	Unit 8 – A
outstanding	/ˌaut'stændɪŋ/	adj.	出众的	Unit 2 – A
overture	/'əuvətjuə/	n.	(歌剧、芭蕾舞、音乐剧等的) 序曲,前奏曲	Unit 8 – B
overwhelm	/ˌəuvə'welm/	vt.	淹没;制服;压倒	Unit 3 – A
owe sth to sb			欠……(某物);应该感谢; 把……归功于	Unit 5 – A
oxygen requirement			需氧量	Unit 4 – A

P

panpipe	/'pænpaɪp/	n.	排箫	Unit 8 – B
passion	/'pæʃən/	n.	激情,热情	Unit 3 – A
patriotism	/'pætrɪətɪzəm/	n.	爱国心,爱国精神	Unit 7 – A
peak	/piːk/	adj.	最高点的,最高水平的	Unit 1 – A
pent-up	/'pent'ʌp/	adj.	被压抑的,被抑制的	Unit 4 – A
perfection	/pə'fekʃən/	n.	完美,完善	Unit 7 – A
permanently	/'pɜːmənəntlɪ/	adv.	永久地;不变地	Unit 4 – B
personal	/'pɜːsənəl/	adj.	个人的	Unit 2 – A

personality	/ˌpɜːsəˈnælɪti/	n.	人格,个性	Unit 3 - A
philosophy	/fiˈlɒsəfi/	n.	哲学	Unit 1 - B
phobia	/ˈfəʊbɪə/	n.	恐惧,厌恶	Unit 4 - B
pianoforte	/pɪˌænəʊˈfɔːti/	n.	钢琴(piano 的旧称)	Unit 8 - B
pit	/pɪt/	n.	深坑	Unit 1 - A
plating	/ˈpleɪtɪŋ/	n.	电镀;被覆金属	Unit 1 - A
plunder	/plʌndə/	vt. & vi.	掠夺;抢劫	Unit 6 - B
policy	/ˈpɒləsɪ/	n.	政策,方针	Unit 8 - A
popularize	/ˈpɒpjʊləraɪz/	v.	使普及; 推广	Unit 7 - B
portable	/ˈpɔːtəbəl/	adj.	便于携带的,手提式的, 轻便的	Unit 6 - A
portion	/ˈpɔːʃən/	n.	一部分,一份	Unit 2 - B
posterity	/pɒsˈterɪti/	n.	子孙,后代	Unit 7 - A
posture	/ˈpɒstʃə/	n.	姿势;态度	Unit 4 - A
potentially	/pəˈtenʃəli/	adv.	潜在地;有可能地	Unit 4 - A
pray for			请求,恳求	Unit 7 - A
precision	/prɪˈsɪʒən/	n.	精确度, 准确(性)	Unit 8 - A
precursor	/prɪˈkɜːsə/	n.	先兆,前兆	Unit 8 - A
predate	/ˈpriːdeɪt/	v.	居先;在日期上早于	Unit 5 - B
preferably	/ˈprefərəbli/	adv.	更适宜地	Unit 4 - A
premier	/ˈpremiə/	adj.	最好的,最重要的	Unit 6 - A
preoccupy	/prɪˈɒkjʊpaɪ/	vt.	占据(某人)思想,使对…… 全神贯注,使专心于	Unit 8 - A
primatologist	/ˌpraɪməˈtɒlədʒɪst/	n.	灵长类行为学家	Unit 3 - A
privatization	/praɪvɪtaɪˈzeɪʃən/	n.	私有化,私人化	Unit 6 - B
privilege	/ˈprɪvɪlɪdʒ/	n.	特权	Unit 7 - A
problematic	/ˌprɒbləˈmætɪk/	adj.	成问题的;有疑问的; 疑难的;未定的	Unit 8 - A
proceed to		v.	接着做某事	Unit 1 - A

professional	/prə'feʃənəl/	adj.	职业的,专业的	
		n.	具有某专业资格的人,	
			专业人士	Unit 5 – A
professional	/prə'feʃənəl/	adj.	专业的	Unit 2 – A
profiteering	/prɒfi'tɪərɪŋ/	n.	暴利,不正当利益	Unit 6 – B
progressive	/prə'gresɪv/	adj.	逐步的;渐次的;	
			循序渐进的	Unit 4 – A
prolonged	/prə'lɒŋd/	adj.	持续很久的,长时间的	Unit 4 – B
prophet	/'prɒfit /	n.	先知,预言者	Unit 7 – A
proponent	/prə'pəʊnənt/	n.	支持者,拥护者	Unit 6 – B
propose	/prə'pəʊz/	vt. & vi.	提议,建议	Unit 6 – A
provoking	/prə'vəʊkɪŋ/	adj.	激怒的,挑动的	Unit 4 – A
puberty	/'pjuːbəti/	n.	青春期	Unit 3 – B
pursue	/pə'sjuː/	vt.	追求,从事	Unit 7 – A

Q

qualify	/'kwɒlɪfaɪ/	v.	(使)具有资格,(使)合格	Unit 1 – A
quasi	/'kweɪzaɪ ,'kwɑːzɪ/	adj.	类似的,准的	Unit 6 – B

R

rap	/ræp/	n.	说唱	Unit 6 – A
rapids	/'ræpɪdz/	n.	激流,湍流	Unit 1 – B
reaction	/rɪ'ækʃən/	n.	反应;回应	Unit 4 – A
reassure	/ˌriːə'ʃʊə/	v.	(使)消除恐惧或疑虑;	
			恢复信心	Unit 1 – A
rebel against			反抗	Unit 3 – B
recorder	/rɪ'kɔːdə/	n.	雷高德(装有舌簧的八孔	
			直笛)	Unit 8 – B
recreation	/rekrɪ'eɪʃən/	n.	娱乐(方式),消遣(方式)	Unit 1 – B

regional	/ˈriːdʒənəl/	adj.	地区的	Unit 2 – A
reject	/rɪˈdʒekt/	vt.	拒绝；摈弃	Unit 4 – A
release	/rɪˈliːs/	vt.	释放；放开	Unit 4 – A
relic	/ˈrelɪk/	n.	遗物；圣物，圣骨	Unit 7 – B
remain	/rɪˈmeɪn/	n.	剩余物；残余	
		vi.	保持；逗留	Unit 5 – A
remove	/rɪˈmuːv/	vt.	移走；排除	Unit 2 – B
renaissance	/rɪˈneɪsəns/	n.	文艺复兴，文艺复兴时期	Unit 8 – B
replacement	/riˈpleɪsmənt/	n.	代替，替换，更换	Unit 8 – B
reputation	/ˌrepjʊˈteɪʃən/	n.	声誉	Unit 2 – A
resident	/ˈrezɪdənt/	n.	居民	Unit 2 – A
resign	/rɪˈzaɪn/	v.	辞去，辞职	Unit 7 – A
resonate	/ˈrezəneɪt/	vi.	产生回声、共鸣或共振	Unit 5 – B
result in			导致，结果是	Unit 7 – B
rhetoric	/ˈretərɪk/	n.	雄辩言辞，虚夸的言辞	Unit 6 – B
rhythm	/ˈrɪðəm/	n.	节奏，韵律	Unit 8 – B
righteousness	/ˈraɪtʃəsnɪs/	n.	正当，正义，正直	Unit 7 – A
ritual	/ˈrɪtʃʊəl/	n.	(宗教等的)仪式；例行公事	Unit 4 – A
routine	/ruːˈtiːn/	n.	例行公事，惯例，惯常的程序	Unit 4 – A

S

salivary gland		n.	唾液腺	Unit 4 – B
satire	/ˈsætaɪə/	n.	讽刺，讥讽，讽刺作品	Unit 6 – B
saxophone	/ˈsæksəfəʊn/	n.	〈音〉萨克斯管	Unit 8 – B
scale	/skeɪl/	n.	鳞，鳞片	Unit 2 – B
schedule	/ˈʃedjuːl/	v.	(时间的)预定，安排	Unit 7 – B
sculpture	/ˈskʌlptʃə/	n.	雕刻，雕塑，雕像	Unit 7 – B

secrete	/sɪˈkriːt/	vt.	(尤指动物或植物器官)分泌;	
			隐匿,隐藏	Unit 4 – B
section	/ˈsekʃən/	n.	部分	Unit 2 – B
secular	/ˈsekjʊlə/	adj.	尘世的;世俗的;非宗教的	Unit 7 – B
sensation	/senˈseɪʃən/	n.	感觉;感受	Unit 4 – A
serenity	/sɪˈrenəti/	n.	安详;宁静	Unit 4 – A
severe	/sɪˈvɪə/	adj.	严重的,剧烈的	Unit 4 – B
shower	/ˈʃaʊə/	n.	淋浴	Unit 4 – A
signaling	/ˈsɪgnəlɪŋ/	n.	打信号,发信号	Unit 8 – B
significance	/sɪgˈnɪfɪkəns/	n.	重大意义,重要性	Unit 2 – B
skateboard	/ˈskeɪtbɔːd/	n.	滑板	Unit 1 – B
sky surfing			空中冲浪滑翔(指在打开	
			降落伞前踩着小冲浪板乘风	
			翱翔的一种特技跳伞)	Unit 1 – B
slang	/slæŋ/	n.	俚语	Unit 1 – A
sleeved	/sliːvd/	adj.	有袖子的	Unit 6 – A
slope	/sləʊp/	n.	倾斜,斜坡	Unit 7 – B
sociologist	/ˌsəʊsɪˈɒlədʒɪst/	n.	社会学家	Unit 6 – A
sociopolitical	/ˌsəʊsɪəʊpəˈlɪtɪkəl/	adj.	社会政治的,同时涉及	
			社会和政治的	Unit 6 – B
soloist	/ˈsəʊləʊɪst/	n.	独奏(或独唱)演员	Unit 8 – B
some sort of			某种;仿佛;多少有些	Unit 3 – A
sonata	/səˈnɑːtə/	n.	奏鸣曲	Unit 8 – B
sophisticated	/səˈfɪstɪkeɪtɪd/	adj.	精密的,复杂的	Unit 8 – B
sophomore	/ˈsɒfəmɔː/	n.	(中等、专科学校或大学的)	
			二年级学生	Unit 1 – A
specialized	/ˈspeʃəlaɪzd/	adj.	专门的,专科的	Unit 1 – B
spectacular	/spekˈtækjʊlə/	adj.	引人注目的;轰动一时的;	
			惊人的	Unit 3 – A

speculate	/ˈspekjʊleɪt/	*vt. & vi.*	思索;猜测,推测	Unit 8 – A
stamp	/stæmp/	*vt. & vi.*	跺脚,顿足	Unit 8 – B
stand	/stænd/	*n.*	看台,观众席	Unit 1 – A
startle	/ˈstɑːtl/	*v.*	使大吃一惊	Unit 1 – A
statue	/ˈstætjuː/	*n.*	雕像,铸像,塑像	Unit 7 – B
steep	/stiːp/	*adj.*	陡的,急剧升降的	Unit 1 – B
step in			干涉,介入	Unit 1 – A
step into			涉足	Unit 2 – A
stereotype	/ˈstɪərɪətaɪp/	*n.*	老套,模式化的见解,成见	Unit 6 – A
stick to			坚持	Unit 7 – A
stimulate	/ˈstɪmjʊleɪt/	*vt.*	刺激;激励	Unit 4 – A
strategy	/ˈstrætɪdʒi/	*n.*	战略;策略	Unit 4 – A
stress	/stres/	*n.*	压力;紧张	Unit 4 – A
stringed	/strɪŋd/	*adj.*	有弦(乐器)的	Unit 8 – B
stunt	/stʌnt/	*n.*	惊人的表演,特技,绝技	Unit 1 – B
subconscious	/sʌbˈkɒnʃəs/	*adj.*	下意识的,潜意识的	Unit 4 – B
subject to			使服从,使遭受	Unit 4 – B
subsequent	/ˈsʌbsɪkwənt/	*adj.*	随后的,继……之后的	Unit 6 – A
substitute	/ˈsʌbstɪtjuːt/	*vt. & vi.*	代替,替换	Unit 6 – B
supplement	/ˈsʌplɪment/	*vt.*	增补	Unit 8 – B
suppress	/səˈpres/	*vt.*	抑制(感情等),忍住;压制; 镇压	Unit 3 – B
survive	/səˈvaɪv/	*vi.*	生存,存活	Unit 2 – A
sustain	/səˈsteɪn/	*vt.*	长期保持;使继续	Unit 5 – A
sutra	/ˈsuːtrə/	*n.*	经文,经典	Unit 7 – B
symbol	/ˈsɪmbəl/	*n.*	象征,标志	Unit 2 – B
symbolize	/ˈsɪmbəlaɪz/	*vt.*	象征;作为……的象征	Unit 2 – B
sympathy	/ˈsɪmpəθi/	*n.*	同情(心)	Unit 4 – A
symphonic poem		*n.*	交响诗	Unit 8 – B

symptom	/'sɪmptəm/	n.	症状;征兆	Unit 4 – A
sync	/sɪŋk/	n.	同时;同步	Unit 5 – B
synthesizer	/'sɪnθɪsaɪzə/	n.	合成器	Unit 8 – B

T

tactic	/'tæktɪk/	n.	方法,策略	Unit 5 – A
take ... seriously			认真对待,严肃对待	Unit 3 – A
take pains			尽心竭力做某事;	
			小心谨慎做某事	Unit 1 – A
take-off			起跳	Unit 1 – A
tantrum	/'tæntrəm/	n.	突然发怒	Unit 4 – B
teenage	/'tiːneɪdʒ/	adj.	青少年的	Unit 3 – B
tempo	/'tempəʊ/	n.	〈意〉〈音〉乐曲的速度	
			或拍子	Unit 5 – B
tendency	/'tendənsi/	n.	倾向,趋势	Unit 2 – A
tension	/'tenʃən/	n.	紧张;张力;拉力	Unit 4 – A
tentative	/'tentətɪv/	adj.	试探性的,试验的,	
			尝试性的	Unit 1 – B
terrorism	/'terərɪzəm/	n.	恐怖主义,恐怖手段	Unit 8 – A
terrorist	/'terərɪst/	n.	恐怖主义者,恐怖分子	Unit 6 – B
the Fab Four			指披头士乐队	Unit 5 – A
theme park		n.	(游乐园中的)主题乐园	Unit 6 – A
therapeutic	/ˌθerə'pjuːtɪk/	adj.	治疗(学)的;疗法的;	
			对身心健康有益的	Unit 5 – B
thrill	/θrɪl/	n.	强烈的兴奋、恐惧或快乐感	Unit 1 – B
timing	/'taɪmɪŋ/	n.	时机	Unit 2 – B
token	/'təʊkən/	n.	表征,记号	Unit 7 – A
tone color			音色	Unit 8 – B
trace back to			追溯到……	Unit 5 – A

trample	/ˈtræmpəl/	vt. & vi.	踩,踏	Unit 6 – B
transcend	/trænˈsend/	vt.	超出,超越;胜过	Unit 3 – A
transition	/trænˈzɪʃən/	n.	过渡;转变;变迁	Unit 8 – B
transitional	/trænˈzɪʃənəl/	adj.	变迁的;过渡期的	Unit 5 – A
transmission	/trænzˈmɪʃən/	n.	传送,传播,传达	Unit 6 – A
treasure	/ˈtreʒə/	n.	珍宝	Unit 2 – A
trial	/ˈtraɪəl/	n.	测试,试验	Unit 1 – A
trigger	/ˈtrɪgə/	vt.	引发,引起(连锁反应)	Unit 4 – A
triumph	/ˈtraɪəmf/	n.	胜利,成功	Unit 3 – A
trivial	/ˈtrɪvɪəl/	adj.	琐碎的,没有价值的, 没有意义的	Unit 4 – B
trombone	/trɒmˈbəʊn/	n.	长号,伸缩长号	Unit 8 – B
troubadour	/ˈtruːbəduə/	n.	行吟诗人,民谣歌手	Unit 8 – B
trumpet	/ˈtrʌmpɪt/	n.	喇叭,小号	Unit 8 – B
tuba	/ˈtjuːbə/	n.	(乐器)大号	Unit 8 – B
tuna	/ˈtjuːnə/	n.	金枪鱼	Unit 3 – A
turn out to be			结果是,原来是	Unit 1 – A
twist	/twɪst/	n.	弯曲;扭歪	Unit 1 – A
typhoon	/taɪˈfuːn/	n.	台风	Unit 2 – B

U

undeniable	/ˌʌndɪˈnaɪəbəl/	adj.	不可否认的	Unit 6 – A
undermine	/ˌʌndəˈmaɪn/	vt.	暗中破坏;逐渐削弱	Unit 4 – A
unique	/juːˈniːk/	adj.	独一无二的,仅有的, 唯一的	Unit 3 – B
unremitting	/ˈʌnrɪˈmɪtɪŋ/	adj.	不懈的	Unit 7 – A
urination	/ˌjʊərɪˈneɪʃn/	n.	排尿	Unit 4 – B

V

veteran	/'vetərən/	n.	老兵;经验丰富的人	Unit 5 – B
via	/'vaɪə/	prep.	经由,经过	Unit 6 – B
viol	/'vaɪəl/	n.	中世纪的六弦提琴	Unit 8 – B
virtuoso	/ˌvɜːtjʊ'əʊzəʊ/	n.	艺术名家,乐器演奏大师	Unit 8 – B
virtuous	/'vɜːtʃʊəs/	adj.	善良的,有道德的	Unit 7 – A
visualization	/ˌvɪzjʊəlaɪ'zeɪʃən/	n.	形象化,想象	Unit 4 – A
vitamin	/'vaɪtəmɪn/	n.	维生素	Unit 4 – A

W

wear the willow			悲悼心爱者的去世	Unit 7 – A
welfare	/'welfeə/	n.	繁荣;福利	Unit 6 – B
western	/'westən/	n.	西部片,西部小说	Unit 3 – A
whistle	/'hwɪsəl/	n.	哨子;汽笛	Unit 8 – B
white-water rafting			激流泛舟	Unit 1 – B
wind-surf	/'wɪndsɜːf/	v.	风帆冲浪	Unit 1 – B
wisdom	/'wɪzdəm/	n.	智慧,知识,学问	Unit 3 – A
World Bank		n.	世界银行	Unit 6 – B

Y

| yell | /jel/ | vt. & vi. | 叫喊 | Unit 4 – A |

根据教育部新的《大学英语课程教学要求》设计编写

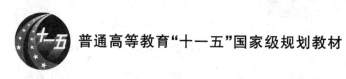 普通高等教育"十一五"国家级规划教材

《大学英语立体化网络化系列教材》

（图书、录音带、配套光盘、电子课件、网络教学系统）

总 顾 问　李赋宁　胡壮麟

总 主 编　黄必康

网络版主编　李建华

《大学英语基础教程》(1-4 册)学生用书/教师用书　　　　　曹杰旺 等主编

《大学英语教程》(1-6 册) 学生用书/教师用书　　　　　　黄必康 等主编

《大学英语阅读教程》(1-4 册)　　　　　　　　　　　　黄必康 等主编

《大学英语快速阅读》(1-4 册)　　　　　　　　　　　　张强乾 等主编

《大学英语快速阅读综合读本》　　　　　　　　　　　　王焱华 等主编

《大学英语视听说教程》(1-4 册)学生用书/教师用书　　　刘红中 等主编

《大学英语实用视听说教程》(1-4 册) 学生用书/教师用书　Jenkins 等主编

《大学英语实用听力教程》(1-4 册)学生用书/录音文本及答案　蒋学清 等主编

《大学英语教程同步测试》(1-4 册)　　　　　　　　　　王焱华 等主编

《大学英语教程学习指导》(1-4 册)　　　　　　　　　　杨 跃 等主编

北京大学 出版社

外语编辑部电话：010-62767347　　　　市场营销部电话：010-62750672

010-62755217

普通高等教育"十一五"国家级规划教材

带你穿越东西文化　助你掌握现代实用英语　帮你步入阅读外刊自如境界

大学美英报刊教材系列

书　名	作　者	定价（元）	书　号 ISBN 978-7-301
美英报刊导读	周学艺 主编	24.00	06165
美英报刊文章选读（上册）（第三版）	周学艺 主编	17.00	00448
美英报刊文章选读（下册）（第三版）	周学艺 主编	17.00	00030
美英报刊文章阅读（精选本）（第三版）	周学艺 主编	36.00	02701
美英报刊文章阅读（精选本）学习辅导（第三版）	周学艺 主编	18.00	03012
当代英汉美英报刊词典	周学艺 主编	52.00	08646
美英报刊阅读教程（高级本）	端木义万 主编	36.00	05005
美英报刊阅读教程（高级本）教学参考手册	端木义万 主编	6.00	05006
美英报刊阅读教程（中级本）（精选版）	端木义万 主编	35.00	08081
美英报刊阅读教程（中级本）（精选版）教学参考手册	端木义万 主编	7.00	08599
大学英语外报外刊阅读教程	端木义万 主编	20.00	05999
大学英语外报外刊阅读教程教学参考手册	端木义万 主编	5.00	06000
体育英语报刊选读	田慧 主编	35.00	11650
新闻英语阅读	[美] Pete Sharma 编	23.00	12146

北京大学 出版社

外语编辑部电话：010-62767347　　市场营销部电话：010-62750672

010-62765014　　邮购部电话：010-62752015

Email：xuwanli50@yahoo.com.cn